Dorothy B Hughes

Henry in a Silver Frame

Henry in a Silver Frame

JAMES EASTWOOD

DAVID McKAY COMPANY, INC.

IVES WASHBURN, INC.

New York

HENRY IN A SILVER FRAME

Copyright © 1972 by James Eastwood

First Published in 1972 in Great Britain
First American Edition 1972

Library of Congress Catalog Card Number: 70-190000

Manufactured in the United States of America

One

Marcello,

You told me to begin at the beginning, and the beginning, I think, must have been that day when I followed her after school. Mine had been the last class. English Literature, the Brontes, I think it was. She jumped on her bicycle and rode quickly, blonde hair flying, through the residential area where the school is, down the main shopping street, past the port and up the hill, and into the grounds of the large, ugly house that is her home.

And I, in my little Morris? I waited, not with any real hope. But with love. When she had stayed behind after the others two days ago, had she really wanted to talk about Heathcliffe and the northern moors? Or simply to be close to me? Had that touch of her hand on mine been entirely accidental? No matter. It had set me on fire, ruined my sleep, inflamed my imagination, triggered action. So now I was following her, secretly, ashamed; already guilty of crimes not yet committed.

The minutes ticked by. Why did I wait? Hoping? For what? Wasn't it enough simply to see my beloved home? To know that she had returned safely to the certainties of family, homework and TV?

Why did I wait, sitting in my little car, smoking my fifth cigarette of the day with quick nervous puffs, expecting ... what?

When, fifteen minutes later, she reappeared, for agonised seconds I did not recognise her. She was no longer wearing the unfeminine, greenish school uniform in which, till now, I had always seen her, but a latest offering of the local teenagers' boutique. Suddenly, she was a stranger from another world, but a creature still more exotic, still more desirable.

She sailed downhill on her bicycle, and again I gave chase, now more the private detective than the jealous lover.

So, like a private detective, I give the exact sequence of events.

Four-fifty. Subject entered a cafe in the busiest part of town. To avoid recognition, I did not follow her inside, but, idiotically, waited outside in the car in what was, of course, a no-parking zone. When questioned by a traffic warden, I said I was having trouble with the motor and, a flustered, helpless woman, was permitted to await the arrival of a mechanic I had not summoned. My first brush with a uniform, with authority. Even then, I was excited, terrified, by my lies, my duplicity. I pretended to tinker with the motor. But of course it would not start – I had disconnected two spark-plug leads!

Five-ten. I reconnected the plugs quickly as subject emerged from the cafe in the company of a youth of about nineteen. Darkly good-looking, his arm around her waist, laughing and running and 'with-it', like a couple advertising something. They ran to a parking lot near by (where she had left her bicycle) and got into a VW painted in psychedelic colours, which the youth drove with great verve. I had great difficulty in both keeping up and not seeming to be following.

Five-thirty. On the coast road. Ours is a very beautiful coastline, Marcello, at least to my way of thinking. The steep, white cliffs, with all their 'sceptred isle' emotional, historical connotations – not Italian, of course, in the least. No white blocks of buildings stark against a blue travel-poster sea. Though they say northern waters are richer in fish than the Mediterranean, somehow one cannot associate our English Channel with *frutta di mare*. The essential greyness persists, even when the sun shines. Along this

6

coast, I have spent many comparatively happy hours, watching sea-birds and sometimes people with the aid of the field-glasses I keep in my little car. (Though my subject is English Lit., I have always been a keen student of natural history, and my only real friend was Miss Kent, the science mistress. It was a great grief to me when she died, last year.) I digress . . .

Five-forty. Subject and her companion left their car at a deserted spot and began scrambling down the cliffs. I parked my car at a discreet distance and followed them, as far as physical courage permitted, field-glasses suspended by their lanyard around my neck. I am terrified by heights. My love was forcing me to a normally impossible act of courage. As I clambered and slid down the cliff, for agonising moments I thought I had lost them, and anyway, would the small stones dislodged by my descent, bouncing on to the beach far below, warn them of my presence? Horror! Humiliation! Yet, breathless, sweating with fear, stockings laddered, hands and knees scratched, I found myself on the safety of a ledge from which I dared not go lower. I listened, at first only to the sea and the cries of gulls. Then I heard their voices . . . By risking neck and detection, I was just able to see them.

Five-fifty-five. They made love. Without any possibility of doubt, my beloved deceived me! Marcello, I saw it all. How she removed her dress, how he took off her bra and panties of a kind (I saw clearly through my field-glasses) I had often touched but not dared to buy at a local store. As she lay there on the rock, I saw her face tense with a passion that seemed like pain; her parted lips, moist, murmuring words I could not hear. And I was sick with envy and desire and shame and fear, fear that I would be discovered as a witness to their love . . .

That, Marcello, was the beginning. Unless you think I should delve deeper, into my childhood, my earliest memories.

The next day I told Miss Dutton-Smith, the head, that I had decided I would like to take a job in the States, a temporary job, of course, and she agreed it would be a most useful professional experience. Miss Dutton-Smith was, in fact, most enthusiastic and co-operative. (She is a great committee-woman and, I think, the 'international' aspect of my request would supply her with good material for her next report to the school governors.)

For the rest of that summer term, I was very brusque with Phyllis (my beloved's name), though she worked hard and became more and more beautiful (because of love?), and won an Oxford Scholarship, and everyone at school was very proud of her.

Phyllis was, I'm sure, astonished and hurt by my change in manner towards her, my favourite pupil. How could she have guessed the real cause! Or how I still constantly thought of her, as on that summer afternoon, helplessly, deliriously subject in the act of love. How could she know that I both loved and hated her? That the teacher had become the fumbling pupil?

That happened last summer. A summer cold and wet, except, it seems now, for that *one* treacherous day; not like this one, hot, suffocating, all over Europe. Unbearable, if one had not thought the temperature was somehow necessary, inevitable, to produce a chemical/psychological reaction.

In the States, as you know, I lasted just seven months. And then we returned on the same boat. In early April. On an Italian boat. You to Napoli – where you were met by your wife and daughter with appropriate enthusiasm – the refugee from a New York 'hell' into which, as you had explained to me on the boat, you thought it necessary to descend, for literary and psychological and sexual reasons, every year or so.

You were returning to Italy, a family, a way of life you apparently found satisfying.

8

I was simply returning. To what?

My old job, with no Phyllis to tantalise my days and inflame my nights?

To him? To Henry in his silver frame, the Henry I told you about during that alcoholic evening three days and nights after we had slid, escaping, under the Verrazano Bridge.

Marcello, you said it would help if I could feel I was writing not just for myself but to someone . . . To you! Did you really mean that? I mean after what happened, or didn't happen, that last night? But you did repeat it just before you went ashore.

'Be honest,' you said. 'Feel every sentence, write about life, feel about it, just as it comes . . .'

Marcello, will you be disgusted with what comes now?

Two

I could see the reporter of the local paper scribbling away, the only one at the press table, his head jerking up and down in a rather hen-like way because of his bifocals, as he glanced at the magistrates or at me, standing there in the dock.

Oddly, I wasn't half as scared as I'd imagined I'd be. Excited, in a strangely physical way, is more the word. The feeling came and went in the pit of my stomach, as if I were on some kind of big dipper. I thought I was going to be sick. But the feeling was almost pleasurable. Psychologically, it wasn't happening to me at all. It was happening to someone else I had sympathy for, and pitied. Yes, and hated.

My solicitor, poor man, had done his best. Of course I hadn't allowed him to call any character witnesses, so he had nothing to fight with, not even a friendly doctor.

The magistrates, three of them, one a woman who looked like a do-gooder with a heart of lead and a blue rinse; a man who looked like a butcher, all florid and red and beefy; and another man with a perpetual, well-practised air of grief, like an undertaker – they whispered together, after consulting the clerk, for all of three minutes before coming to their decision.

It was blue-rinse who did the talking.

'Elizabeth Edwardes' – the voice was squeakily censorious – 'you have pleaded guilty and no extenuating circumstances, no medical or psychiatric evidence, have been placed before us to explain why you, a woman of education and background, have committed this offence. The fact that you are a teacher, a person with young and impressionable girls in your care, adds to the gravity of the matter. It is true that you have expressed your profound regret and said that you acted solely because of a sudden, uncontrollable impulse. It is true that goods are tantalisingly displayed in many stores. But temptations of this kind must be resisted. By every woman. And especially a woman who has a standing in her community. A teacher!'

Blue-rinse spoke with such feelings that I imagined she must have been often tempted herself!

'We have to consider also the ingenious way in which you attempted to take the goods out of the store. On your person! An attempt thwarted only by the vigilance and professional skill of the store detective.' (Through the corner of my eye, I could see the woman who had given most of the evidence for the prosecution looking smug, self-satisfied. Didn't she care, didn't anyone care about me at all! Oh God, can't anyone help me to understand myself! Why am I dying, inch by inch?) 'The stores must be protected. Society must be protected. Most of all, the young girls in your care must be protected. Offences of this kind are far too prevalent. An example must be made.' (My legs are jelly. Who is holding my arms? To prevent me from falling?) 'A term of imprisonment would, we feel, be justified in your case. However, in view of your profession and the grave effects on your career which will inevitably follow this conviction, we feel that your punishment will go further than anything this court could inflict. But if you come before us again on a similar charge and are found guilty, imprisonment will then be inevitable. You will now pay a fine of £25.'

Blue-rinse had become breathless and quite emotional.

'Thank you,' I said, in a voice I only faintly recognised as my own.

The undertaker said, 'Do you wish time to pay?'

'No, thank you. I have the money.'

Someone touched my shoulder and guided me from the

11

dock or I would have stayed there for ever. Then I was standing in a room filled with policemen without helmets, all carefully not looking at me, counting out twenty-five pound notes, just half the fifty I'd drawn from the bank the previous day.

Then, suddenly, I was breathing free air. I took great lungfulls of it. I just stood there, gasping, like a landed fish, hoping someone would throw me back.

Then I saw him. The reporter, the one with the bifocals, getting into his car, a very old mini. And suddenly the idea came. I knew I had only seconds.

'Hullo!' I said, as stupid a way of starting as any. 'I suppose I'll make the front page?'

He looked up at me from the driving-seat, sheepish, compromised, like a man caught by his wife talking to a whore.

'You'll have your place.'

'Must I? I mean, is it necessary?'

'Duty of the press and all that.' He had a Welsh accent and a gold crown. And a wedding ring. He looked about thirty-five and harassed. I had always imagined reporters to be cool, unruffled, flinty.

I said, 'It isn't even as if I lived in this town. I'm not local news. You know where I live. Eastcliffe. Fifty miles away.'

He pressed the starter and the engine sounded, when at last it started, very rough. 'Your car's as old as mine,' I said. 'You could do with a new one.'

He felt for a cigarette, his right foot pumping the gas-pedal. I didn't know whether it was to gain time, to prevent any curious passer-by overhearing what we were saying, or simply to coax the engine to run smoothly.

'Your story could make the nationals,' he said. 'Easily.'

'And then of course you'd be paid accordingly?'

'Look,' he said, 'I can't go on talking to you like this. I'm

12

a reporter, I have a job to do, and that's all there is to it.' His hand moved to the gear-lever.

'Please,' I said. 'Anything.' I felt more humiliated than I had in court.

He inched the car forward.

'Please,' I said again.

'There's a pub around the corner. The Crown. Ten minutes.'

I watched the car go, belching blue smoke. I hurried to the pub which was just opening. (My case had been the first on the list.) I went in with indecent haste, like an alcoholic seeking his first drink of the day.

Is that what the barmaid thought as I downed a large gin and tonic? Or was she somehow already aware of my so recently proclaimed guilt? Did it *show*? There was a mirror behind the bar. I stared at myself and thought, no, I didn't look like a criminal. But I remember my father telling me – he was a clergyman – that sooner or later sin would always show. But for the moment, I was just a schoolma'am in a sensible tweed suit, altogether too hot for the time of the year. I was, in fact, sweating. But I had anticipated jail, and this seemed the most suitable garb to go to prison in. I was hot, but shivering uncontrollably.

'You all right, dear?'

I pushed my empty glass towards the barmaid.

'I must have caught a chill,' I said. 'Have one yourself.'

'Well, thanks. I'll have the same.' She seemed surprised. Probably women didn't often buy her a drink. 'You're down from London for the day.'

'Yes, on business,' I lied.

I had my eye on the clock. Seven minutes gone. She served my drink and took her time getting her own. I put a five-pound note on the bar, taking it from an envelope containing fourteen more.

'Oh, what line are you in?' she asked, her eyes on the money.

13

'Underwear. Self-service stores,' I said, to say something, anything, yet keeping as close to the truth as possible. I giggled. The gin was already doing its therapeutic work.

I was glad when she moved away to serve another customer who had just come in. Not him! A full ten minutes now. He probably wouldn't come, had just wanted to get rid of me. At this very moment, most likely, he was at his desk at the newspaper writing my case up, for the early editions.

In that case I wanted to be out of town as quickly as possible. I finished my second drink at a gulp as the barmaid came back with my change.

'Must rush,' I said, sliding off the stool. The certainty of full exposure now upon me. My guilt broadcast. Guilty, guilty! Anyway, it was Friday and I should have been at school, talking, at that precise moment, to the Upper Fourth about the Lake Poets. I had to escape, and, anyway, there are times, often, when I have to escape though I am guilty of nothing; when I run from shops, restaurants, anywhere where there are people. Sometimes, though I have been teaching for years, facing a class is torture, and I have rushed out in the middle of a lesson – just to be alone in the loo . . .

I was already at the door, thrusting the change into my purse.

'You!'

I bumped into him, almost blindly, as I rushed from the pub.

'I said ten minutes.'

'You're late. Do you want to go in, or shall we talk somewhere else?'

'You'd like to go somewhere else?' He was watching more carefully, more openly than he had outside the court.

'Yes.' I didn't want to face that barmaid again.

'All right. I'm not a regular in this place. But one never

knows who one might meet and...'

'You wouldn't want to be seen talking to me. I quite understand. I'll walk behind you to the car.'

He drove to a detached, undesirable house on a newish estate on the edge of town, with a lawn that needed mowing and a rusty child's tricycle near the front door. But we went in through the back.

There was a pile of dirty dishes in the kitchen sink, a quantity of odoriferous empty cans and two or three bottles which had once contained Spanish Burgundy.

'Well, it isn't much,' he said. 'But it's home.'

'How long ago?' I said. 'I mean when did she leave you?'

'Exactly three months ago, yesterday.'

'Taking the child with her?'

'Two. Aged three and five. All back to mother.'

'Where's that?'

'Spain. Malaga.'

'Romantic!'

'Very!'

'That's where you met her?'

'While enjoying "two sun-drenched weeks beside an azure sea". I quote.'

I took off the jacket of my pre-prison tweed suit, still feeling unbearably hot, though the shivers had subsided. 'You'd mind if I tidied up a bit?'

'Dish-washing! Now there's a novel way to subvert the press.'

'Not really. I simply find it easier to talk if I'm doing something.' I filled the sink with hot water.

'Personally, I find talking easier if I have a glass in my hand.' He uncorked a new bottle of red biddy. 'It's all I've got. Since paying their fares home and sending them something every month, can't really afford gin.'

He was talking about money, which was encouraging.

'She was home-sick?'

15

'That and other things. For example, I hadn't enough *panache*, it seems. She's crazy about matadors, thinks them very sexy. Once I stuffed a large handkerchief down the front of my pants – which I'm told they do to add to the illusion of masculinity – and I sometimes tried to cook *paella* to the best of my ability with the materials available locally. But she wasn't impressed.'

'That was soon after she arrived?'

'Yes. We had our wires crossed from the start. I thought I was marrying a sexy maiden-of-the-sun and that there'd be the sound of guitars and the scent of oranges every time I looked at her. She thought she was marrying an English gent. Though actually I'm Welsh, as you may have noticed, and my father was a miner. It's extraordinary how snobbish Continentals can be about the British. You'd think we still had an Empire!'

'Well, *this* of course.' He raised his glass and emptied it. 'And the fact that I'm a reporter. Not enough togetherness. Though she always managed to give the impression when we were together she couldn't stand the sight of me.'

'Still, you gave her a nice home.'

'And I'm still paying for it, plus most of the furniture.'

Good, he was talking about money again.

'We ought to talk business,' I said.

'I can't keep your name out of the local rag,' he said. 'I'd lose my job. Your case is the best court story of the week. Everything else this morning was petty traffic offences.'

'So you left the court when I did to get back to the paper?'

'Yes.'

'Then if you can't keep me out, why did you meet me?'

He helped himself to more wine and filled a glass for me. His furtive look had come back. He said, 'Well, there's the question, as I hinted to you, of the Sundays.'

'You mean, you could keep me out of those and keep

16

your job at the same time?'

'You'll keep *your* job after this?'

'I don't know. Perhaps if the story can be kept local and the people at home never know . . .'

'You like being a teacher?' he said.

'Sometimes. Not often. I often have the idea I'd like to break away, do something really exciting.'

'Then why don't you? You're not bad-looking, not bad at all.' I realised he was looking at my breasts, and blushed. 'Actually, I'm not too keen on reporting, I mean the kind of reporting I do, on a local paper. I like really using words. I'm really another Welsh poet. Unpublished, of course.'

'Why?'

'Because my name happens to be Thomas. Well, that's as good an excuse as any. Most of my poems aren't actually written anyway. They're floating somewhere at the bottom of a bottle.'

'What would a Sunday newspaper actually pay for a story about me?'

'Well, now, that depends.'

'On what?'

'The precise details.'

'You heard them in court.'

'The evidence was a bit vague. The prosecution talked about goods stolen to the value of £5. What kind of goods?'

'This is an interview?'

'A business discussion. I have to know what I have to sell – or not sell. As you decide. "School Teacher Shop-Lifts" is an interesting story. But what, and why? There could be material for a juicy background article.'

I said, 'I have £75 on me in cash. I'll send you another £75 on Monday when I've failed to find anything about me in the Sunday papers.' I was surprised how cool I suddenly sounded.

I let the water out of the sink and dried my hands.

He said, 'The store detective happens to be a friend of

mine. I can get any additional information I need from her.'

I was not supplicant any more, just angry. 'Then why don't you?'

'Well, we did have a brief chat. While you were paying your fine. Undergarments, she said. Now I wonder what kind?'

'That's important?' I said icily.

'Ladies' undergarments are always important,' he said. 'What would the press and the ad-men do without them!' He refilled his glass. 'The flimsy stuff, of course. Bikini briefs, a shortie nightdress, things like that.'

I could see he knew. I opened my purse and put the fourteen fives on the top of the refrigerator.

'You seem to have all the information you need,' I said. 'Now I have to be going.'

He looked at the money but didn't touch it. He said, 'I know teachers aren't paid much, but why didn't you simply buy the things?'

'Don't people usually want something for nothing?'

'Not people like you.' He was still looking at the money. 'Your sort like to pay their way. What made you do it? I mean that particular kind of sexy stuff? You're not a teenager doing it for kicks. You're not a middle-aged house-wife at the change of life. You're thirty-three and, as I said, not bad-looking. So why?'

I made to pick up my jacket, but he took it first.

'Why?' he said again.

'Just pick up the money,' I said.

'The whole thing would be a lot less unsavoury – and more lucrative – if we collaborated.'

'Collaborated?'

'I mean your own story in your own words, suitably edited by me, of course. I have a features editor chum in Fleet Street who would be very receptive.'

'No. May I have my jacket, please?'

18

He didn't give it to me. 'You're going to need money, aren't you? We split, fifty-fifty.'

For some reason, at that moment, I felt a sort of kinship with him. Marcello, was it because I had met another tortured, self-destructive misfit, like myself? Did he understand already, about my crimes past, my crimes-to-be, committed or, morally as indefensible, merely planned?

'You want to cut loose,' he was saying. 'Now's the time. You'll probably be cut loose anyway.'

I said, 'Given the guts and the opportunity, what would be your sin?'

'Sin? Now that's a word one doesn't hear often these days.'

'I'm a clergyman's daughter. Now there's a piquant detail for your story. A non-conformist clergyman from the North. He's dead, so anything you publish can't hurt. You're quite right in thinking I'm some kind of freak. I was carefully brought up. I teach girls of sixteen who take the pill and, at thirty-three I'm practically a . . .'

I couldn't bring myself to utter the word. Virgin! After all, it's something no one is these days. It's rather comical, like saying you've never been on a bus or eaten spaghetti.

'I thought so,' he said. 'You poor thing . . . you poor thing.'

He was staring at me. With pity!

Tears were close, but I stormed at him, 'There's your story. Isn't it good stuff! "Pupils teach teacher about sex." Print whatever you like. And damn you!'

All the pent-up emotion was now flooding out.

He did the banal thing and handed me a not very clean handkerchief. 'Look,' he said, 'why don't you go upstairs and freshen up. The bathroom's the second door on the right.'

I fled upstairs, past the bullfight poster on the landing, glimpsed an unmade double bed, with a Spanish embroidered bedspread, and a crucifix above it on the wall. Evidently he had done his best, after his fashion, to be assimi-lated.

For seconds I stood before the basin sobbing, then bathed my face in cold water and groped for a towel.

When I opened my eyes he was there behind me, so close it was impossible to escape.

'No,' I whispered. 'Please.'

Perhaps the second word, contradicting the first, had sounded like an entreaty. Perhaps it was meant to be. I mean subconsciously. I don't know.

I turned to face him directly. He grabbed my shoulders almost roughly and I could feel him hard and insistent against my groin.

Then I began to struggle. He tried to crush his mouth against mine, but I clenched my teeth and moved my head spasmodically from side to side. His fingers sought the buttons of my blouse. But I didn't want him. I was terrified of the male organ, terrified of being pregnant. I didn't want him, or any man.

After a while he let go of me and he said something, I suppose, in Welsh, and then, 'All right, all right. Keep it.'

I said, 'I don't want pity.'

'You don't want experience. Of sex, or anything else.'

He turned abruptly and left the bathroom and I heard him going downstairs.

Again I repaired the damage to my face.

Back in the kitchen, he helped me on with my jacket, but we did not look at each other. He took another glass of wine and lit a cigarette.

'I'll drive you to the station.'

'It doesn't matter. Aren't we on a bus route?'

'Yes. But it's a poor service. I'll drive you.'

'No. I'd rather not.'

'Don't argue about that,' he said. 'I have to go to the office anyway.'

I glanced at him then, and he looked, I thought, suddenly

20

like a small boy who had been chastised for improper be-
haviour, and I felt a sort of pity for him mingling with the
contempt I felt for myself.

'I'm sorry,' I said.

'Sorry? *You're* sorry?'

'For being childish . . .' I fumbled for the words. 'It, it's
the way I am. Look, give me a big drink, and let's go back
upstairs.'

'No,' he said. 'I couldn't now. Really. Thanks all the
same.'

We didn't speak all the way to the station.

I held out my hand. 'Good-bye.' I said.

'Good-bye.'

I glanced at the station clock. Just after 1 p.m. By this
time I could easily have been either in bed, or on my way to
prison. I shivered and bought a first-class ticket, the only
way I could think of at the moment of recovering my
dignity.

At the bookstall, I bought a 'homes' magazine, *Cosmopolitan, Forum,* and of course the early edition of the local
evening paper. To pay for them, I opened my purse.

I saw at once the fourteen crisp new £5 notes. He must
have returned them while I was still upstairs.

There was nothing about me in that early edition, which
wasn't surprising as there hadn't been time to get the story
printed. There was nothing about me, I could discover, in
any of the national newspapers the following day, Saturday.
And nothing on Sunday, even in the tabloids. The whole
week-end in my little cottage, I wallowed in newsprint
searching.

Nothing.

By Sunday evening, I was beginning to feel human again
and, sipping gin and tonic, went over my notes on Defoe,
wondering just what I should say about Moll Flanders – a
character in fiction I have always envied – in case any girl

21

in the Lower Fifth should ask. (My subject would of course be *Robinson Crusoe*. Much safer!)

Now and again I would glance at Henry, looking out at me from his silver frame. Henry, my dear fiance who always writes to me once a month, sending me of course his mother's regards.

Why doesn't the old bitch die? I was thinking, just as the phone rang.

'Ah, Miss Edwardes! I was afraid you might be indisposed.'

Miss Dutton-Smith's voice. My head-mistress! Horrors! I had completely forgotten to ring her up and give some explanation for my absence from school last Friday.

'Well, I have been a little unwell, Miss Dutton-Smith. I'm sorry I didn't ring you earlier to explain.'

'Oh dear. I'm so sorry. You're better now?'

'Yes, quite better thank you.'

'Oh, good, good...' A slight pause, a clearing of the throat. 'Miss Edwardes, what I was really phoning to tell you is that there will be no need for you to attend morning prayers on Monday.'

'Not attend prayers, Miss Dutton-Smith?' I gasped. It was like excommunication.

'Perhaps you would be so kind as to come and see me in my office. At say nine-thirty ...?' A click.

She knew!

22

Three

Let me say at once that Miss Dutton-Smith in my many but brief contacts with her, has invariably filled me with presentiments of impending doom. My head-mistress had the softly gentle, unbelievably waxy, but oddly sinister immobility of a supposedly lifeless figure in a wax museum who turns out to be human after all, and who has been putting on an act to scare the paying customers. There at her desk she would sit, totally frozen for interminable seconds, as one wondered if one should send for the doctor or the undertaker. And then she would come to sudden, radiant life, straight from the Chamber of Morals.

Miss Dutton-Smith was fixed in one of her immobile moments now. It had been established that we had both enjoyed and been refreshed by our week-ends, and I waited, anxiously gazing at her face. I was no longer in a museum. I was in a church. Would there be a miracle? Would blood or tears flow down those waxen cheeks?

I was not disappointed. There was a moistness around the corner of the left eye. The lips moved.

'My dear Miss Edwardes, you have nothing to tell me, nothing to say?'

I tried to look co-operative, questioning, penitent.

'About Sixth-Form English?'

The tear consolidated itself and ran down Miss Dutton-Smith's cheek.

'My dear child, you must think what you owe to me, yourself, the school.'

I was the sinful novice before the mother superior. Obviously confession, abject and total, was the only salvation.

'You are referring, Miss Dutton-Smith, to my conviction?' I tried to make it sound matter-of-fact, an everyday subject of conversation. Conviction, convictions. Matters of belief. Faith, hope, charity and, of course, forgiveness.

'But why?' Miss Dutton-Smith murmured. 'A woman of your sensitivity, your intelligence, your academic attainments, your achievements with the girls! Why?'

Why indeed! If Miss Dutton-Smith could for a moment imagine the real reason: that I had been frustrated in my attempt to seduce one of them, her beloved girls! But how did she know about my crime?

Via the establishment grape-vine? The magistrate with the blue rinse? The press, with encouragement, had failed to do its duty. The 'protect-our-girls' league certainly had not.

'There must be a reason!' Miss Dutton-Smith was saying. 'Your father, a clergyman . . . your background . . .'

'Exactly!' I said, suddenly angry, tired of guilt. 'My father and his background. That about sums it up.'

'You blame him, that good man?'

'I don't blame anyone. I was born. I did what I suppose I was destined to do. I was found guilty, I paid the fine and was set free. I discharged my debt to society. I'm sorry it happened, but now please can't we forget?'

'Forget? Yes, and forgive. But what about your future?'

I was sorry to see her embarrassed by her pain. I write glibly about Miss Dutton-Smith, but I really liked her, and I think she liked me. Sisters in suffering? With your total ignorance of the English scene, can you understand that, Marcello?

She is older, much older. Probably she has become resigned. But she calls it devotion. Devotion to the school, to brisk walks on the Downs, and home for scones and jam and tea and correspondence, interspersed with carefully chosen programmes, of cultural significance, on TV.

Is she what I want to become, in twenty years? Sleeping

in my meticulously kept house between solitary lavendered sheets, and eating dietically sound, vitamin-correct meals for one? Is that what I want?

'Miss Dutton-Smith,' I said, 'I see it now, very clearly. When I stole, did something criminal, I was, subconsciously, if you like, destroying my future. I mean as a reluctant member of a dying race. Haven't we outlived our usefulness? Does anyone *need* unmarried, dedicated virgins to look after their children any more? We survive. But don't we really belong to the remote past? Somewhere before 1939?'

I was a little shocked at myself. I had said 'we', including her in my guilt.

Miss Dutton-Smith, however, did not appear to have noticed. She said, 'I thought you were engaged to be married.'

'I thought so, too. But I've been engaged for eight years.'

'A long time. I'm sorry. Please go on.'

'Haven't I said more than enough?'

'I find everything you say extremely interesting.'

'Interesting?'

'Of course. You have touched on matters to which I have in fact given considerable thought. I have to confess that there are, possibly, girls in this school – even fourteen-year-olds – who know more about "life", as sex is sometimes called, than I do. A few of them take drugs. Many have seen *Hair*. They all go to the cinema and see what is to be seen in the cinema these days. In spite of all our efforts to interest them in the arts, the sciences, the professions, though many will go to the university, in the end the majority will become housewives. A significant proportion of those housewives will, in time, become divorced. One sometimes wonders if all this educational effort is worth while. But then, of course, there is the occasional brilliant, gifted girl, and one has the answer.'

It was my turn to freeze into waxed immobility. After what seemed a long silence, I said, 'I'm afraid I'm simply not good enough, not dedicated enough.'

'Oh, you're good enough,' Miss Dutton-Smith said. 'But you must try to understand that there are many kinds of love. Anyway, I think you need a change, a new perspective. The present matter is out of my hands. The Governors, not to mention the parents ... I'm sure you understand. I'm sorry.'

I didn't understand. Not fully. Not then. I stood up. So did she.

I said, 'Please don't apologise for having to fire me.'

'Let's call it resigning, shall we?'

'I just want to go somewhere and hide.'

'That would be a great waste. You mustn't imagine this is the end of everything. Life isn't contained within these school walls.'

It wasn't! Ask the boss of any institution: prison, hospital, government department, political party, commercial enterprise, trade union, *school*! Yet *you* say it, Miss Dutton-Smith! Astonishing, incredible!

The waxen face smiled. The dun-coloured, purely perambulatory legs moved to a cupboard I had, on previous visits to this hallowed study, imagined to contain only the reports of commissions, the findings of learned bodies, the entombed minutes of defunct deliberative assemblies, the dossiers of past students who were probably already grandmothers. Instead of some file, however, the pale hands brought forth a bottle of Manzanilla and two crystal glasses which were filled to within an inch of the brim.

'It is a little early in the morning for sherry,' Miss Dutton-Smith said. 'But then the circumstances are a little unusual.'

She raised her glass and I raised mine. Salutation and farewell.

'I wish you joy in finding whatever it is you seek.'

'I wish I could say something that wasn't banal, something that would express my gratitude for your kindness adequately.'

'Today, nothing could be banal,' Miss Dutton-Smith said. 'As it happens, it's my birthday. I'm fifty.'

I looked at that waxen skin and wondered, for the first time, why I had seen so little of her recently around the school. Not long ago, she seemed to be everywhere at once, showing fantastic energy. Was she simply tired? Or more than tired?

'Many, many happy returns,' I said, for want of anything better.

'One would be happy with three hundred and sixty-five days. Still, with Piaf, one can say *Je ne regrette rien* – though our activities have, of course, been in rather different fields. You are surprised to hear me mention Piaf?'

'Frankly, yes, Miss Dutton-Smith. You surprise me more with every second that passes.'

'I am a great lover of France. I go there every summer. Or used to. Everyone has a dream country. Which is yours?'

'Italy,' I said.

She smiled and nodded. 'Dream countries do not exist. But it is important to have the dream.' Suddenly she was brisk. 'You have personal belongings here?'

'Only a few.'

'I would prefer if you ...'

'Just faded away. Yes of course. I'll leave by the side entrance.'

So I stole away, like the thief that I was, Miss Dutton-Smith's kiss of parting still damp on my cheek, absolved, but still guilt-ridden. And yet, in a curious way, I was elated; I had an extraordinary sense of release. I had a double gin and tonic to steady my nerves and to celebrate at a pub near the school, never before entered for the sake of the proprieties.

Marcello, can one really be born again?

A compulsion to tidy things up before departure. I busied myself about the house, then decided to do something about money.

A professional woman, a teacher no less, I have always been a privileged customer at the bank. Marvellous credit-rating. A reliable pillar of society and all that.

Mr Askey, the manager (who obviously hasn't *heard*) gives me that friendly but business-like handshake, that father-figure smile so much publicised by all the banks, and after a breezy chat which takes in his recent holiday in the Pyrenees, the state of the national economy (a hint of warning here), and the future of youth (pessimistically hopeful, he has a daughter, not very bright, at school), he asks what he can do for me.

Well, now! Since Mr Askey is about forty-five, a widower in comfortable circumstances and apparently good physical condition, there is obviously a lot he could do for me. But why isn't he re-married, at forty-five? Can he have problems, too?

In the brief moment before I am admitted to his sanctum, he has asked for my financial record and the papers are now spread before him on his impressive, but otherwise uncluttered desk. The computer has revealed all; my average balance on current and deposit accounts over the past ten years, my salary, the fact that I have never been in the red, my very financial soul! The ideal manager meets the ideal customer – who does not really need money.

Since leaving Miss Dutton-Smith I am in a state of shock; numb, but with a compulsion to talk.

Is there something about me a little strange? Why is he looking at me a little oddly.

'Well, now, what *is* the problem?' His smile suggests every problem can be solved by the bank.

28

'The problem is, simply, that I am unhappy.'

The smile fades fractionally, but the bonhomie heroically persists. Unnecessarily, Mr Askey glances at the record before him. 'Unhappy, eh? Well, I see you have never called upon our quite impressive resources before – and you're an old customer. Just the sort of person we like to help. What do you need to make you happy? A dishwasher, a new car, colour TV?'

I tell you, Marcello, one couldn't wish for a nicer bank manager.

'None of those things!'

'No? Then what do you need to cheer you up?'

'Mr Askey, my problem is quite simple. I'm lonely.'

His attention suddenly appears to become concentrated on a document he had until this moment unaccountably overlooked. The kind man is giving me a few moments to overlook my indiscretion. I wait patiently for his spasm of diplomatic deafness to pass.

'Ah, do forgive me. You don't actually seem to need money, Miss Edwardes. You have in fact quite a respectable balance, and your salary cheque is of course paid in regularly. However, if there is some special emergency...?'

'Mr Askey,' I say patiently, 'I told you. I don't actually need money. Not at the moment, anyway. Though who knows?'

'Who indeed!'

'Especially as I've resigned my job.'

I thought that would make him sit up. It does.

'Resigned, did you say?'

'Effective immediately.'

'In the middle of term?' He stares at me as if he has to do with a mad woman, which may well be the case.

'Yes. I've decided to give up teaching. I'm starting an entirely new life.'

'New life? But teachers get such long holidays.'

'Long holidays aren't enough, Mr Askey. Haven't you

29

ever longed to get away from the bank, right away? And to hell with the pension!'

Mr Askey draws on all his reserves of tact. 'A career in banking has a lot to recommend it,' he says. 'One meets so many different kinds of people.'

'But not many like me, I imagine? A spinster of thirty-three abandoning her career.'

'May I ask a personal question, Miss Edwardes?'

'Of course!'

'Why aren't you married?'

Ah, a direct attack. The best form of defence.

'I could ask you the same question.'

'No, no, Miss Edwardes. Forgive me, but you came to me with a problem, not I to you.'

'Touche!'

'Marriage,' he said, 'is supposed to be a sovereign cure for loneliness.'

'I have a fiance.'

'Ah!'

'I've had him for nearly eight years.'

'Then may I suggest you make other arrangements. Miss Edwardes, we at the bank have found our existence quite transformed by the computer.'

'Yes, I can imagine. But . . .'

'Think, Miss Edwardes, if the computer can perform miracles for the bank, imagine what it could, possibly, do for you.'

'You're suggesting I try computerised dating?'

'Well, since your fiance seems, shall we say, disappointing, it might be worth a trial.'

'You've given it a try?'

'My dear Miss Edwardes!'

'I'm sorry. Do forgive me.'

'Affairs of the heart are not, as I'm sure you appreciate, within the competence of the bank.'

'You mean love?'

'Well, yes.'

'But doesn't love lead to marriage, and doesn't marriage lead to a family and all its attendant responsibilities: loans, mortgages, overdrafts, wills, insurances. Money, Mr Askey. Money!'

'Well, put that way of course . . .'

'So that's why I came to you. I had to talk to someone.'

'You don't have friends, Miss Edwardes?'

'No, I'm lonely. I told you. Believe me, I wouldn't be talking to you if I hadn't had a couple of gins before coming in to see you. I'm very unfashionable. Not one of your swinging youngsters whose money the bank is so anxious to get its hands . . . I mean to have as customers. But I do probably have a bigger balance.'

'But no longer a secure job!' He stared at the ceiling. 'Miss Edwardes, have you never considered making contact with a reputable matrimonial agency?'

'No. It seemed so cold-blooded.'

'Then what about taking a cruise?'

'And all those romantic tropical nights? I did take a sort of cruise, actually, when I came back from America this spring. Cabin class. The passengers were mostly middle-aged couples, and most of the time I was sea-sick. But there was a man who showed some interest.'

'There! You see!'

'An Italian.'

'Oh really?' Mr Askey wrinkles his nose in polite interest, as if I had mentioned garlic. Marcello, I apologise. But he is a club-tied Englishman of a dying race.

'A Roman,' I added. 'Very dark, sophisticated, middle-aged. A writer. I talked to him a lot during the voyage, about my personal problems. He advised *me* to write.'

'Write to him?'

'Yes. But not for him.'

'I'm sorry. I don't follow.'

'He meant I should write a novel.'

31

'You have literary aspirations?'

'I don't know. But aren't all good novels supposed to be written by unhappy men – and woman?'

'Well, if writing gets it out of the system...' Mr Askey is advocating the merits of a patent medicine? 'Anyway, this Roman gentleman was evidently good for you.'

'Oh, very! I think! Especially on the last night of the voyage, after the gala dinner. I must have drunk a whole bottle of champagne.'

'Oh, good! Nothing like getting a little tiddly once in a while, as the Chinese say, or whoever ...' Mr Askey suddenly remembers his managerial majesty. 'Quite!'

'They had to put me to bed.'

'They?'

'There was some help, I seem to remember, from a steward. But truly and honestly, I don't remember exactly what happened. Just Marcello sort of manoeuvring me into my cabin.'

'Marcello, eh?'

'The Roman's name ... The next morning I discovered I wasn't the same girl.'

'Oh really? I'm afraid I don't quite ...'

'I mean, you know ... well, I wasn't a virgin any more. It's not that I minded. Far from it. I just wish I had been conscious enough to enjoy it.'

Mr Askey blushes deeply. He clears his throat. 'Err ...'

'Oh dear, I do hope I haven't embarrassed you. But I simply had to talk to someone, and who better than my friendly neighbourhood bank manager?'

'Well, perhaps. The bank's range of services is very wide, but I scarcely think your particular problem ...'

'Falls within your province.'

Mr Askey shifts uneasily in his chair. No hope for me here.

'Miss Edwardes, I am glad, sincerely, that we had this little chat. If there is anything, anything at all, you think

32

the bank can do for you, please call on me. Don't hesitate. Any time.'

Mr Askey starts to rise, indicating that his time is valuable. He offers his hand, like a priest to a mourner. Warm, comforting, accompanied by a look of intense benevolence – employed how many times, after refusing a loan?

Suddenly, unexpectedly, his rather nice, doggy eyes focus on mine.

'My dear Miss Edwardes, may I give you a little advice?'

'Oh, please!'

'Strictly off the record, of course.'

Breathless, I await the oracle.

'Go away, Miss Edwardes! Go away from this town, and sin some more!'

I fancy Mr Askey winks. Where, I wonder, does he do his sinning? I have the distinct impression that I have made his day.

I withdrew from my account £300 in traveller's cheques, practically my whole balance, and returned to my tiny cottage on the edge of town, with its dust-sheeted furniture. Everything ready for absence, departure.

If not to jail, then where?

The bed looked inviting. After Miss Dutton-Smith's call I had scarcely slept, and the gins (djinns?) were beginning to catch up on me. The temptation to slip between the cool sheets was almost irresistible. But I knew that, if I succumbed, my resolution would be gone. If I was going, it had to be now.

I picked up the phone and ordered a cab, then started to pack. Just one case, the bare essentials.

Less than an hour later I was on the train, to London. I slept? Confused, disorientated, arriving at Victoria, I felt sucked into a great vortex of people. Individuals? Yes. But mindless as myself, attempting admittance or expulsion from the metropolis. Trying to fight free, I found myself in

33

the Continental Arrivals area, where the language ceased to be English but became French, German, Italian, and tongues I did not recognise at all. Evidently a train from Dover had recently arrived. Women, some nursing small babies, crouched resigned but not terrified against the grimy walls ... Indian women, Pakistanis ... waiting for a relative who would carry them off in a second-hand car to the paradise of Notting Hill or Bradford or Sheffield. How far off did Calcutta or Karachi seem to these women now... ? Who was I to think I had problems?

There are those whose lot it is to arrive; those who must depart. I hardened my resolution.

The taxi-driver said, 'Where to?'

'An hotel. At London Airport.'

'Heathrow? That'll be three quid.'

He was looking at me as if I couldn't afford the money. 'All right.'

'Which hotel?'

'I don't mind. It doesn't matter.'

'They all cost around six pounds a night.'

'So?' I said haughtily.

'So it's your money,' he said. 'I've a daughter who looks a lot like you. A teacher!'

I didn't actually dislike the man. But I didn't speak a word to him the whole journey.

The reception area of the hotel was filled with men wearing what I recognised as Brooks Bros-type suits, who had evidently just flown in from the States, hostessed (the right word, I believe) by two girls wearing plastic smiles on plastic faces and the kind of clothes that looked as if they had been moulded to their figures, accentuating every quiver of their shapely behinds. I was madly envious. I was in the big, wide, jet-set world. This was it. An airport hotel. The way out!

The clerk at Reception looked at me in exactly the same

way a steward had done on the ship when accidentally I had strayed from Cabin into First.

'Yes?' Cold and frosty.

'I'd like a room.'

'A room?' He appeared astonished.

'For one night. This *is* an hotel?' My most acidulous voice, as if I were addressing a particularly obtuse pupil.

'You have a reservation?'

'No, I don't.'

'Then a room is, I'm afraid, quite impossible. We're fully booked.'

I had an almost irresistible desire to slap his face. Like many shy, vulnerable people, I suppose, I do have these violent urges. He turned away.

An American voice said, 'You're sure you can't give this little lady a room?'

He was around thirty-five, I guessed, very well-groomed, with a little card in his button-hole that said, *'Hi, I'm Elmer Hackensack.'*

The clerk turned. 'I'm sorry, sir. A room is really quite out of the question.' The voice, however, was much mellower.

'No kidding?'

'Absolutely not, sir.'

As I picked up my bag and moved away from the desk I realised, not without anticipation, that Elmer seemed to be following me.

Across the crowded exit, I said, 'Well, thanks, anyway,' and added, as if an after-thought, 'Hank.' Americans were, I supposed, matey.

'Elmer,' he said.

'Okay,' I said. 'Elmer.'

He was looking at me with a little-boy-lost look. 'Say, listen,' he said, 'you can have my room.'

I stared at him. What does a newly emancipated but *nice* girl say under such circumstances? Yes, please! Well,

35

maybe! Or simply smile?

I simply gulped and said nothing. But I must have appeared vaguely affirmative.

'Number 103,' he said, producing the key. 'There's ice, an almost full bottle of Johnnie Walker Black Label and a copy of *The Sensuous Male*. Help yourself.'

The key, held between finger and thumb, swung six inches from my nose like a hypnotising bauble.

I couldn't think of an utterable word.

'Baby,' he said, 'if this hotel is full, you can be sure there won't be another vacant room within miles. What are you waiting for?'

There was a wedding ring on his third finger left hand. But perhaps he was divorced. Now that would be a new life. Out West, across the Atlantic. He had soft, smooth skin, like a girl. Why wasn't he a girl?

'Where are you from, Hank, I mean Elmer?'

'Huh?'

'I said, "Where are you from?" Isn't that supposed to be the opener?' The truth is that, after months in the States, I had met, talked to scarcely anyone, apart from the kids themselves of course and their parents and other teachers. All that snow in the Middle West! It limited contacts.

'From?' Elmer said. 'Denver, if you must know. It's important?'

'No, it isn't. Of course not.'

'Then why ask, baby?' The crowd was thinning, a bus and the two hostesses, waiting. 'Look,' he said, 'I gotta go. You want the key? Yes or no?'

I stretched out my hand and took the bait, regretting that my nightie wasn't exactly what I would have shop-lifted for the occasion. (The stolen goods I had given back!) 'That's sweet of you!' I was uncertain about the idiom. Anyway, perhaps he would be more thrilled by an English Miss.

'You bet!'

'I'm Liz Edwardes,' I said, thinking it was only right to

36

be introduced, as it were, to the man I was going to sleep with.

'Hi, Liz!' he said, squeezing my hand but looking towards the crowd of disappearing Brooks Bros suits. 'Be seeing you.'

He merged with the other suits, disappeared towards the bus. I stood there, in the now almost empty reception area, holding the key. I walked diffidently, as if I were guilty of something, towards the lift.

It was a very pleasant room: low-key lighting, TV, Elmer's suitcase open and his dressing-gown, bright orange, hung inside the bathroom door. The perfect comfort capsule, except there was no man. I helped myself to a large Johnnie Walker, drank, and discovered that I was crying. The fatigue of a long day? If I was going to be a hip modern miss, this would never do.

Anyway, what did people actually do, apart from sleep and make love in such rooms? They made executive-style decisions, that's what!

I picked up the phone. 'I'd like to make a plane reservation.'

'Which airline?' the girl said as if I'd been ordering coffee, black or white.

'Alitalia,' I said. Which else, Marcello?

A moment later, a voice said, 'Alitalia. Reservations!'

'I wish,' I said, very cool, sophisticated, 'to book a ticket on your first available flight tomorrow to Rome. One way.'

Ten minutes later, in spite of brief blandishments of verbal sensuous masculinity, I was asleep. With nightmares. In some vast prison, cell doors clanged. A face zoomed in immense close-up towards mine. 'Take a bath!' I plunged into a chipped, filthy tub with six inches of water, but it turned out to be so deep that I almost drowned and didn't know if I was swimming up or down, but, finally, lungs bursting, I surfaced and cried out, screamed, in both terror and relief ... Someone was holding my

37

shoulders and saying, as if from an immense distance, words I didn't understand.

A face came and went. Finally I recognised Elmer, bending over me like a male nurse.

'Take it easy,' he was saying. 'Take it easy.'

I didn't know where I was. I remembered nothing but, briefly, the sweaty memory of a nightmare. Then I did remember. This strange man, looking down at me, looking down at me with intimacy, yes intimacy on his girlish face.

'Something's wrong. I know something's wrong ... I wish I could stay and help. But I have to go ...'

'Go?' I was desperate, an only friend departing.

I jerked up in bed, saw he was fully dressed, his bag near the door.

'Brussels,' he said. 'The convention moves on. It's only seven. The room is yours – till noon. The bill's paid.'

I slumped back on to the pillow. God knows how much of the Black Label I must have drunk. I dozed off. When I came round again it was after nine.

Treading barefooted around the room, I found a $50 bill. An offering to an unused whore? Or a token of help – to a little sister?

I picked up the phone and asked for breakfast. Waiting, I found a postcard, a picture of the hotel. And in my suitcase, to my surprise, I found that I had packed the silver-framed photograph of Henry.

More to fill in the time while waiting for breakfast than for any other reason I could think of at the moment, I decided to write to him.

'Dear Henry! I am leaving for Rome. Do you care for me at all? Elizabeth.'

My plane left at eleven.

Four

In sending a postcard to Henry, I was, I suppose, guilty of both provocation and keeping the options open. Suppose you weren't in Rome, Marcello, to receive me? Suppose you had given me a fictitious address? Suppose you didn't exist at all, that I'd simply invented you? After all, aren't the people one meets on boats creatures who exist out of time, without past, without future? One promises to write, hopes to meet again, parts with affection, even sometimes with love. But the voyage is really like a chapter in one's life that doesn't belong. In trying to see you again, Marcello, was I attempting the impossible, pretending that two total strangers were really friends?

What was I doing on that plane? Why were all the other passengers going to Rome, anyway? Why was anyone going anywhere?

At the end of the runway as the plane paused before take-off, I was seized by a wild panic. I wanted to get off, to run away, screaming, across the vastness of the airport. Only the belt and the embarrassment of appearing a fool in front of the other passengers, prevented me from rushing to the door.

I glanced at the man in the next seat. He was already engrossed in papers from his briefcase. He might have been sitting in a train, even his office. And he was about to fly! To experience one of man's oldest dreams become a reality!

Marcello, in this day and age! It was my first flight.

The rush down the runway engulfed me in pleasurable terror. And my fellow-passenger was still reading! I watched houses, factories become children's playthings, and southern England become a map. Then I began to relax and enjoy it, helped by the ministrations of Alitalia's cabin staff. After a time, even I began to read: the current *Cosmopolitan*, a journal which, I confess, started me off, psychologically, on my career as a swinger, liberating me, while I was still in the States, into the uncharted oceans of 'with-it', orgasmic, unvirginal femininity, except that I was still at sea – or rather in the air – an eager but still unfulfilled stowaway.

Somewhere over Elba, I think, the man in the next seat offered me a cigarette, told me he was going to Rome for some kind of sales conference, that he flew somewhere or other in Europe three times a week, and would I have dinner with him that evening at, say, Alfredos where the *fetuccini* was out of this world. 'Let's share a taxi,' he said. 'Taxis in Rome are always a gladiatorial struggle.'

I can't say I wasn't flattered, but I declined both offers politely and said friends would be meeting me. (Marcello, I didn't want to be mixed up with another *Englishman*!) But at Fiumicino it was 85 in the shade, there was of course no one to meet me, and I rather regretted the kind man's offer. I boarded the bus, was deposited at the central air terminal where I politely joined what I thought, naively, was a queue for taxis. But after half an hour of being jostled, elbowed and trodden upon, I began to see what the Englishman meant about a circus.

Then I heard another English voice saying, in female accents one can only describe as colonial, 'It's absolutely no use queueing or you'll be here all night. *Boy!*'

She was angular, about sixty, said she lived in Bermuda ('How can *anyone* live in England these days, though of course I always regard it as home!'), and was brandishing a thousand-lire note. A porter took the note and a taxi materialised which I was glad to share. The memsahib alighted at the Excelsior Hotel which I was determined not to enter, even if they had a room, as my funds, though absent from home for little more than twenty-four hours, were vanishing at an alarming rate.

'Take me,' I said to the driver who spoke broken American and had a brother-in-law in the Bronx, 'to Trastevere. The Pensione Fratelli.'

The *pensione* you had suggested, Marcello – remember? – if ever I came to Rome. Did it exist? The driver doubted it, and after we crossed the Tiber asked the driver of every other taxi halted beside us in the city's incredible snarl-up.

But suddenly there the place was, in a street just wide enough to take the cab, and I began to believe in the reality of your existence, too, Marcello. But frankly! after one glance at the exterior, I wanted to flee. Back to the certainty of almost any hotel, no matter how expensive. Back even to the welcoming wings of Alitalia to fly me back, at a nod, to, well, what ...?

Trying to analyse my terror, I can only imagine it was that closed, shuttered look the place had. I did not want to knock on a strange door in a strange land, to cease to be a mere cosseted tourist.

The cab-driver was still waiting. I could jump back inside his cab and run. And regret it for the rest of my life.

I paid the man and knocked on the strange door. A bent old woman, thin and tough, at last appeared, looked at me suspiciously, but, when, phrase-book in hand, I mentioned your name, Marcello, she said she would fetch the signora.

The signora was fat and also suspicious, and said something I didn't understand at the time, about another signorina americana. I said I wasn't American, but she seemed to regard this as a mere quibble. The room, anyway, would be three thousand lire a night, and the shower was the other side of the courtyard.

How long would I be staying?

Marcello, how long? A few days, a month, a lifetime?

In the room, which was simple, but adequately clean and holy – Madonna over the bed – I assessed my resources. After paying for my ticket (single), taxis and miscellaneous expenses inevitable when travelling, I had parted with nearly £60. Leaving £240. Enough for how long? Two months? Three if I were frugal? There was of course also Elmer's $50.

But that, I decided, was for some catastrophic emergency, such as breaking a leg. Unpacking, I had put Henry's photo in its silver frame on the bedside table (God knows why!). I now took the photo out of the frame and hid the $50 between the photo and its backing. After which, I reframed Henry. He and Elmer, my ultimate guardians, people of last resource!

Quite suddenly, I was exhausted. I opened the bottle of Scotch which I had been unable to resist buying, duty-free, on the plane. I poured a good three fingers, sipped, undressed, put on my dressing-gown and lay on the lumpy mattress, listening to the machine-gun splutterings of the motor-scooters, the shrieks of children, the maniacal ravings of a sports commentator coming from at least a dozen radios and TVs in the immediate vicinity of the *pensione*, and tried to sleep – while brooding over the possibilities of my new life.

Legitimate, gainful activities? Well, what were my qualifications?

A degree in Eng. Lit. 2nd Class Hons. That would, presumably, enable me to apply for some post as teacher of the language at some academy that used the direct method only. (My knowledge of Italian was confined to the first two pages of 'Everyday Expressions' in the phrase-book.)

But I didn't want to be a teacher of English or anything else. Again? Why *else* had I escaped?

Secretary? There would be English and American companies in Rome looking for girl-Fridays, and I can type. But that would be a sort of compromise. Not a true release.

Anyway, they'd probably want someone bi-lingual, if the ads in the *Rome Daily American* I'd read on the plane were anything to go by.

What then? Dubbing at Cinecitta? After all, I had once helped to produce a school play (*Lady Windermere's Fan* – all schoolgirl cast) so I could claim theatrical experience. But that seemed a bit of a cliche thing to do, and I'm not of course actressy. Wouldn't I have to sleep with someone to get a job?

So what remained? I could work in a shop near the Via Veneto and sell shoes or handbags to Anglo-Saxon tourists, matching my ignorance of Italian with their own? Perish the thought.

There had to be something more exciting. Well, what about crime? After all, I was a criminal, with a record to prove it. Didn't the international underworld – the Mafia! – have its origins over here? Surely *they* could use an innocent-looking (deceptive) young woman, as a courier, possibly, in some hazardous but lucrative enterprise? Well, why not?

Imagining myself meeting a Sicilian gentleman in the manager's office of a Roman night-club and being handed a heavily sealed envelope and an air ticket to New York – or was it Hong Kong? – I fell asleep. And dreamed ... I was being chased by Thomas, or whatever-his-name-was, right into the printing presses of his newspaper, revolving at whirlpool like speed, dragging me towards them. I was wearing only a very short nightie, naturally, and the men tending the presses laughed obscenely as the nightie was pulled up around my shoulders as I was caught by it in the revolving press. And there I was, caught in the rollers, about to be spread, quite literally, all over the front page ... and I woke up, bathed in the sweat of terror, but not to full wakefulness.

The room was dark now and I didn't know where I was. I knew nothing except that I must have been mad ever to have left home. Such a pleasant little home, all chintzy and snug and safe. Why struggle? Why not accept the obvious? ... It was just then that the music started. A violin and an accordion and a very passable liquid-sounding tenor, singing, *O sole mio*, or *Sorrento* or something equally banal, and I just lay there and let the sound wash over me. Yet it wasn't banal, somehow. It was like the sound-track of a film, the music that gives significance to, say a man walking down a deserted street. Nothing in itself, but perhaps the most important thing he does in his whole life.

A little later, I got up, opened the shutters and looked out into the street that had seemed so squalid when I arrived when it was still daylight.

Fantastic transformation! As magical as that which takes place when the lights on a stage or film-set go up, turning a rather depressing arrangement of plywood and canvas into a living, important focal point, concentrating a moment, an experience, a life. Phoney, irrelevant, but somehow a means to truth, as, sometimes, I had had insights about myself, my work, when reading something trivial and quite unrelated. Suddenly, knowing yet not knowing, I knew why I had come to Rome.

The music came from the restaurant at the end of the street, *in* the street now, with its romantically lit tables, operatic waiters and, of course, the tourists, mostly Americans, seeing exactly what they had come to Italy to see. Eating lamb flavoured with rosemary to the sound of music and a splashing fountain. The essence of the package tour, what it was all about.

The smell of the food made me hungry, and, fifteen minutes later, I was in the restaurant myself, at a table for one, feeling happy and miserable, hungry, but unable to eat.

Should I call you now, Marcello? Or wait till morning?

I picked at the lamb, took frequent sips of wine. Were

44

the couple at the next table whispering about me? Did the waiters think I was just another peculiar English miss in search of a quickie love affair in Rome?

Of course. My waiter, slim with burning eyes, serving me as if I were a princess incognito, told me that his name was Alberto and that he had worked in London and found English girls *simpatico*; and the second half-carafe he brought unasked, was on him, and he would be off duty in an hour. He had, he said, worked also in Brussels and Frankfurt and New York. But there was nowhere like Rome. Would I give him the honour to allow him to show me Rome? He flashed his liquid eyes.

'Thank you,' I said, frostily, 'but I just dropped in for a quick meal. I'd like to use your phone.'

If it hadn't been for Alberto I probably wouldn't have phoned you that night. Perhaps never.

The phone was on the bar, inside the restaurant, near the kitchen door. Alberto followed me and, seeing that I was unfamiliar with the mechanics of making a call, got your number for me. He then hovered within ear-shot.

'*Pronto!*'

Your voice! Butterflies in my stomach as well as un-digested lamb. For a moment I could not speak. Also, I was a little drunk.

'*Pronto!*' you said again. Irritated?

'Marcello?' I managed to get out in an almost inaudible croak. 'This is Elizabeth.'

'Who?'

'The Leonardo da Vinci. Remember?'

'Ah!' Long pause. Were you delving into memory? How many Anglo-Saxons did you sleep with on that voyage, Marcello? Seven nights, seven women? Or maybe more? After all, you were apparently the only unattached man on board. 'Elizabeth?'

'Blue eyes,' I said. 'Brown hair, five foot seven, uneven

45

teeth, and' (hating the admission, but how else to bring myself to mind) 'a schoolteacher, from England. Remember?'

I might also have added 'the virgin', more significantly, but Alberto was still hovering and there are limits to public confession.

'*Elizabeth!* You're here? In Rome?' You sounded incredulous.

'I flew in a couple of hours ago. You were the first person I just had to see!'

'Well, that's wonderful. Where are you staying?'

'Guess. You should know.'

It was very hot, so close to the kitchen. I was sweating, and not only because of the heat. Alberto placed a glass of wine at my elbow and also offered me an immaculately clean handkerchief soaked in cologne. (Did he know *all* my secrets?) Gratefully, I dabbed my forehead and the back of my neck. (How different would this story have been if I had taken up with him?)

'I should?' This after a long silence.

'Well, of course. The Pensione Fratelli. The place you recommended. Where else? Just around the corner, I think you said, from your flat. I'm speaking from a restaurant on the corner. The trattoria ...?'

'Minerva,' Alberto put in helpfully.

'You've already eaten?'

'Yes.'

'You have!' Marcello, I fancied you sounded relieved. (Frankness, always, remember?) 'Well, why don't you come round for a drink?'

'Now?'

'As soon as you like.'

I hung up trembling, quite faint. Alberto followed me to the doorway. 'If it doesn't work out, signorina ...'

I fled.

46

Marcello, I found your flat above the wine shop, just a few yards from the news-kiosk – exactly as you had described it on the boat – without difficulty. But when you opened the door, for a second I thought I had the wrong address. I did not see the well-tailored Don Juan of Cabin Class, but a biblical prophet with cotton robe and spindly legs and hair to shoulders, gazing at me as if exhorting me to repentance, or perhaps to some new sin. Or was it simply continuing non-recognition?

But you kissed me, as if I were a holy object, on both cheeks, slowly, ceremoniously. 'Welcome!' you said. 'Truly welcome. I was sure that, one day, you would arrive.' You placed your hand upon my forehead in a guru-like gesture. 'It was ordained!'

Softly repeated chords on strings, Vivaldi in sombre mood, came from inside your flat. You led me down the corridor, as if I were an initiate, to a room lit only by a ruby-glass-shielded candle.

Dusty! My first glimpse of you!

A glass of wine balanced on your stomach as you lay there on the divan, nude. The incense, I came to know later, was pot. I could not see your face, but your body brought a shock of delight and recognition. I thought I was seeing Phyllis again.

Nothing was said. Nothing seemed to be necessary. I had simply completed the trio.

I sat down and listened to the music. You handed me a 'cigarette'. As I gazed at her, I became more and more aware of a piece of sticking plaster on Dusty's right cheek, and what appeared to be a bruise on her forehead.

'Dusty's political,' you said.

'Political?'

'That's how she got the cut and the bruise. She was in the demo this afternoon. She was hit.'

'By the pigs!' Dusty said. 'My first decorations!' She turned to face me in a sinuous, animal-like movement. 'But

47

it doesn't really count. The place to protest is home – wherever home happens to be. This afternoon I was hoping to be arrested, but the moment the cop discovered I wasn't Italian but American, he pinched my bottom and let me go. No international complications. You're English?'

'Yes.'

'I thought you looked a bit tense. I mean tense personally. Though from what I hear, there isn't enough real tension in English politics these days, I mean, about the things that count.'

'Such as?'

'Putting an end to the consumer society.'

'Many people in England are only just starting to consume. It makes a pleasant change.'

'But the consumer merely becomes a factor in the economic system. He exists to consume. By consuming he digs his own grave. He ceases to exist as a person. Against this one must protest.'

'Dusty's father is one of the richest lawyers in New York,' you said. 'She protests in comfort.'

'That's unfair,' she said, 'and you know it. My attitude would be exactly the same if my father were white trash or black.'

'Except then you'd be a different person, a different you.'

'Probably even more violent.'

'And violence leads to jail.'

'Good. Some of my best friends have been in jail. Some still are. When I get back home I'd like to give a report on what conditions are like in Italian jails. But it's difficult to get in, even though I am of Italian stock. Third generation. Remote, but I still have chianti in the bloodstream. Some of the kids here have the right ideas. But a lot of them are Catholics. I'm not sure you can worship the Pope and Chairman Mao at the same time. Today the only true Commies are in China, don't you agree? Long live the

48

thoughts of Chairman Mao!'

'You wouldn't like to live there,' you said. 'Not in China.'

'That's true. I'm far too interested in love. Or should I say sex? I'm already corrupted. I feel for Daddy! He was terribly upset when I was arrested back home.'

'You were in jail there?'

'Only for a few hours. Not enough to get the feel of the place. He had me sprung, against my vociferous protests, naturally. I was furious. I mean going to jail is an experience everyone should have. Absolutely seminal. Why do I always talk in sexual terms, even negatively? I did flirt with a way-out woman's lib thing in the States for a time. But it wasn't really for me. I mean, I don't go for this theory that clitoral stimulation is as fulfilling and orgasmic as the vaginal variety. Protest has its limits.'

You said, 'I think you're embarrassing Miss Edwardes.'

'Oh, stuff! You've slept with him, of course?'

'Yes, I have, haven't I, Marcello?'

You inclined your head as if I had asked for and been given absolution.

'And that's why you came to Rome? Why all his women, the non-Italians, turn up here sooner or later. They come to see what he's like on home-ground. Have you many female acquaintances you haven't slept with, Marcello?'

'Not many.'

'You see,' Dusty said to me, 'he has this theory: he can't write about women unless he's had them. Has he told you you ought to write a book? He has? Me, too! And show him the results? I tell you, he's a manipulator. And how!' Dusty rose from the divan in a single sinuous movement and entwined her arms around your neck. '*Amore mio*. I have to go.'

'Another demonstration tomorrow?'

'You're jealous?'

'Just curious.'

49

'Well, who said curiosity is the mainspring of love? Or did I just make it up? Anyway, if you don't see me tomorrow – do they allow women to have visitors in jail?'

I said, 'If you're so anxious to be inside, why not perform some simple criminal act? Rob someone, preferably with violence.'

'I've thought of that,' she said. 'The robbery doesn't matter. An apparently motiveless crime has its attractions. Crime as an art form?'

'Yes. I suppose you could put it that way.'

'The ultimate form of protest. Though it would be nice to think that someone benefited?'

'The Robin Hood syndrome.'

I glanced at you, Marcello. You were wearing your sleepy lizard look of course, but you were anything but asleep. Dusty disengaged herself, put on her panties, then slipped into a long sack-like garment which, though shapeless, looked exactly right on her. Her feet remained bare.

As she moved to the door, I said, 'Have you ever done anything really violent?'

'To people? A person?'

'Yes.'

'I've kicked and punched a few cops who were, I'm sorry to say, too tough or too well-padded to feel anything. But it got me arrested.'

'You enjoy violence?' you said.

'I think it's sometimes necessary.'

'I mean, does it give you a kick?'

'I'd do almost anything for kicks,' Dusty said.

She moved away from the door, back to me. Looked at me, just as Phyllis had looked, asking some silly question or other about the Lake Poets.

'Why don't you take your clothes off?' she said. 'You look as if you need sort of liberating. Nudity helps, believe me.'

'My body isn't as good as yours.'

50

'That doesn't matter. Where are you staying? The Pensione Fratelli?'

'Yes.'

'Where else!' She pinched your cheek. 'That's where you put up all your girl-friends, don't you, *amore mio*?'

And then she kissed me, not on the cheek, but full on the mouth. 'We'll be seeing a lot of each other then?'

'Yes, I suppose so.'

My pulse was racing. After she left, we scarcely spoke, you remember, Marcello? We simply sat there in your study, looking at one another.

Any word, at that moment, would have been an indiscretion. True. But was it in that moment that you conceived *the idea*?

I was aware that someone had entered the room. Very silently – not with the wish to catch us unawares, but simply because quietness was natural to her.

My first and lasting impression of your wife, Marcello, was of her strangely ethereal beauty, and I could imagine her listening to her patients with almost saint-like detachment, acknowledging the existence of no sin that was not also a sickness.

And yet, and yet... Why did I feel as she joined us, that it was not as a detached observer but as a fellow-conspirator?

She kissed you, in wifely fashion. By me, I think, at first she was a little puzzled. Was I so very different from your usual conquests?

After a few moments of banal chat, Clara went to the kitchen. 'She never eats between breakfast and supper on her clinic days,' you told me. 'You like our little American?'

'She is very interesting. Yes. She is very beautiful. You are in love with her?'

'Perhaps a little. I am forty-five. I find it revitalising to

51

keep in touch with the young.'

'Because you are a writer?'

'And because I'm a man. As a teacher, you don't have this problem.'

'On the contrary. They are strangers to me. I envy them. I am afraid of them.'

'Including our little American?'

'She especially, though I know nothing about her. I can't imagine why.'

'Then you must see more of her, as of course you will. You have already eaten, you said?'

'Yes.'

'Then you will excuse me if I eat with Clara? A small domestic convention we still adhere to.'

'Of course.'

Dismissed, I imagined, I rose.

'Watch us eat, if you like.'

'No, no.' Perhaps Dusty would already be back at the *pensione*.

'How is Henry? Henry! That was the name you mentioned, I think, when we talked on the boat?'

'Yes. Henry is still in his silver frame.'

You nodded. 'Of course, or you would not be here.'

I hurried back to the *pensione*, but the key to room 4 was on the rack, unclaimed. I waited half an hour, then took a Mogadon and waited for a Roman dawn.

Five

The next morning somehow the need to find a job didn't seem urgent any more. Surfacing from sleep, the first thing I saw was my portable typewriter, lid off, a challenge. If I wanted to write, I should write. And there you were, a professional, ready with advice! If my work didn't sell, not to worry. Wasn't it possible to live in Italy on very little money? Or even in America if I joined one of the communes in, say, Californa? Or what about a kibbutz in Israel?

And yet, and yet... Was it what I really wanted? For such a change, wasn't I too English, too old?

Wasn't coming to Rome, to you, only an attempt to see things in perspective before returning 'home' (wherever that was) to the real battle-ground? Wasn't anything else merely running away?

But mostly I was thinking about Dusty.

I went to her room. The bed had been slept in, the sheets were still warm from her body. A glass was lipstick stained. There was an empty bottle that had contained milk. Already she was out in the world as I lay sleeping. Out in the city.

When I went out myself, half an hour later, was I looking for her? Trying to protect her from herself?

Around the Colosseum, at the Piazza di Spagna, the Trevi Fountains, wherever I went, there were truck-loads of police. Police smoking, reading newspapers, listening to the radio, a little self-conscious, perhaps, as they were being stared at by tourists getting a little more excitement out of their trip than they had paid for.

Half a million people on strike. Trouble in Calabria. Militant students. And the temperature stood at ninety-two. There was a possibility of a general strike.

The middle-aged American couple at the next table in the cafe to which I had retreated for a lemonade, worried about the possibly of returning home to Chicago the following day. Perhaps the airport would be closed.

An obviously American couple, clothes, cameras, sensible, sight-seeing shoes, package-tour, credit-card protected, amoured-by-passport-against-involvement aliens.

He would be around fifty and on the tour of a lifetime. Do it now! See Europe while you can, while it lasts!

When a line of students marched down the street past the cafe, the man rushed into the street, camera whirring, keen to get some shots that would really make them sit up at home. Medium cool in Rome. And I don't mean Rome, N.Y., or Rome, Georgia. I mean Rome *Italy*!

A youth shouted, 'Yankee, go home!'

The tourist aimed his camera at him. Close-up of protesting youth. 'Whatsa matter! You don't like dollars any more?'

The students hammed a scene for the tourist, taking the mickey. Then someone tried to grab his camera. There was a scuffle.

Suddenly the tourist was on the hot asphalt and the boots were going in.

'Brad!' His wife charged to her life-partner's assistance, armed with a sunshade. An effective weapon, but not effective enough. Within seconds, she was down and I saw a girl kicking her.

I didn't 'decide' to do anything, but suddenly I was a part of the struggling mass of bodies, clawing the woman and her husband, trying to drag them free.

I didn't know them or like them. I simply didn't want to see them get hurt. It didn't look that way to the police. In the fight that followed, I hit out at demonstrators and men in uniform alike. Then, suddenly, as the struggle fragmented, like a breaking wave, I was running. Not alone.

54

When I fell, someone dragged me to my feet and, still clutching my arm, made me keep on running till I thought I'd drop.

Then I was in a courtyard, the shouting, the traffic noise muted, and someone was bathing my face in the marvellously cool water of the fountain.

A young woman said, 'You're feeling better now? You're English?'

I nodded, too breathless to speak.

'I saw what you did. Some of the youngsters get out of hand. But in what they really think, what they feel, they're right! You're a teacher?'

'It shows?'

'One can usually tell. There are housewives, women, and *teachers*. They have a dedicated look. I teach history, but I try to get in some politics. You're active?'

'Politically? No, not really.'

'A pity. Children need guidance, if only to counteract the influence of the home and church. In every country, there is a lot that has to be changed. In East and West. Those who try to run things for their own selfish ends must be made to realise that we cannot compromise. Anyone who stands in the way of freedom must be neutralised, or at least discredited. Not just politicians, but parents, fiances, even husbands and wives who tacitly support the system. You're married?

'No.'

'Good. Even if you think you need a child for some biological or psychological reason, a husband isn't necessary and can be a nuisance. There is work to be done, and I don't mean housework. The home is no longer a woman's prison. In Italy especially, women have much to learn ... In England, too?'

'People everywhere have a lot to learn.'

She looked at me very seriously. 'I said "women". I think you are perhaps, as they say, "dodging the issue"?

You must see things clearly, then fight for your freedom. I think it is quieter now. It is safe for you to go ...'

Strangely elated, I returned to the *pensione*. I was delighted to find Dusty, wearing jeans, lying on my bed, drinking my Scotch.

'Hi!' she said. 'I hope you don't mind my being here.'

'Of course not.'

'But this was Sally's room.'

'Sally?'

'Marcello's last girl-friend but three, from Pueblo, Colorado. We exchanged notes, she got jealous and left. Don't you think jealousy stupid and unethical?'

'Probably.'

'You,' she said, 'look as if you've had a tough day.'

'Tough and exhilarating.' I told her all about it.

'Good,' she said. 'You were battered by life. I was hit by a blast from a water-cannon. Quite useful, really, as the shower here isn't working because of the strike. Tomorrow I'll take the soap along. There's a trickle here, though. I used your soap and cologne. I hope you don't mind.'

'Of course not.'

'Go ahead and change. Don't mind me.'

'But I do "mind" you,' I said.

'Okay, that makes it more interesting.'

I started to undress.

'You've a good body,' she said. 'Something he's particular about. Did you make love last night?'

'No ...'

'Because you thought it a bit embarrassing with his wife around?'

'Well, partly that, I suppose.'

'You don't have to worry about her.'

'Oh?'

'Well, she's one of the few really intelligent wives. Of course her profession helps.'

56

'A psychiatrist?'

'Yes. It makes her very understanding.'

'Of course there was another reason. He didn't ask me, or want me. Because of you?'

'Possibly. We were making love when you called.'

'You mean...'

'Yes, screwing. For the second time that day. And twice a day is just about his limit, I've discovered, after diligent research. He's good but he has his limits.'

'You met him in the States?'

'At school, in Vermont. He came to give a talk on Dante. God knows why I went, seeing my subject is biology. Anyway, after the talk, during which I was thrilled by his person, I discovered where he was staying and went to see him at his hotel. I talked to him in Italian. "Signore, you are just about the most exciting man I ever saw in my whole life," I said, or words to that effect. He was just about to leave for the airport, but he cancelled his reservation, phoned Chicago, his next lecture stop (which cost him, I'd imagine at least $100 in loss of fees), and we put his luggage into my VW and drove to the nearest motel where we spent two whole days and nights. He said I was especially valuable to him because I was the youngest girl he'd ever had.'

'When was this?'

'Last fall. I was sixteen, but of course I could make myself up to look twenty, which I did for the benefit of the folks who ran the motel. But once in the room, I was sixteen again, for him. It was fab.' She took another pull at the Scotch, watching me performing the more intimate part of my toilet as I sprayed my under-arms and what the ads call the most girl part of you.

'When did you make his acquaintance?'

'On the boat, coming back to Europe.'

'That would be soon after he said good-bye to me.'

'Yes.'

57

'Well, he's positively not monagamous. But I don't give a damn! He's getting sort of older and I want to give him any help I can.'

'Help?'

'I mean in his work. He's a fine writer. Or so they tell me. Or should I say, as *he* tells me! Conceited, of course, but what creative person isn't? And hasn't the right to be! It's a shame he's never been a success in the States. He's just too Italian, I suppose. What do you like about him most? His brain or his body?'

I stood before her nude, consciously provocative.

I said, 'I'm not very experienced in men's bodies. In fact, I've always felt a sort of distaste. I don't know, perhaps because of ...'

'Something to do with your father?'

'I suppose so. Yes.'

I began, reluctantly, to dress.

'I knew a girl like that once. Mary. Mary never had dates. But Mary made a pass at me, though.'

'And what happened?' I asked, my mouth dry.

'We made love, sort of.'

'Pleasurably?'

'Well, it wasn't distasteful, exactly.'

'Then exactly what?'

'I say, you do have some square clothes!'

'I do?'

'You don't mind if I went with you shopping?'

'I'd like that.'

'D'you mind if I ask a personal question?'

I shook my head.

'On the boat, before you knew him were you ...?'

'Yes,' I said.

Dusty got off the bed, came over to me and kissed my cheek. But chastely. 'He's special,' she said.

'Well, he is to me, anyway. He's why I came to Rome.'

'Me, too. Because he makes life more interesting?

Because he has a sort of radiance? Sometimes, I think, he *glows*. He's a kind of saint. He's special.'

'Special?'

'Last week-end we went down to his cottage on the coast. Marcello, Clara and me. We went swimming and on the beach he found a piece of driftwood shaped like a big, rough, knobbly letter Y, as big as himself, and he picked it up and, carrying it across his shoulders, it was as if it were a cross and he walked with it back to the village. It was a real Via Dolorosa, him naked except for his swim trunks, so boney and lean and beautiful, and his long prophet's hair. It must have been all of a mile, but he carried his heavy cross all that way. And there were all these Italians in the village, sitting on the walls of those narrow streets, and he kept blessing them as if he were on the way to his crucifixion. It was comic and pathetic and it was beautiful. I laughed till the tears came, and that night when he made love to me, it was as if I was taking part in a sort of rite, something almost religious. He has lots of other girls down there, too.'

'Oh?' I said, my mouth like dry leather.

'Spending the summer, waiting for the schools to open. They come to that little white house of his as if to a chapel, and he talks to them about love and true communism. It's very, very beautiful. Very late that same night he wrote a poem about me and his wife, Clara, made a sketch of me – yes, she's a real artist – and somehow I felt, you know, *created*! As if for the first time in my life, I really began to exist!'

'What was the poem about, Dusty?'

'Gosh, I can't remember. But it sounded beautiful, a sort of incantation.'

'What happened to the cross?'

'He was going to hang it on the wall of his white house.'

'As a relic?'

'He says nature makes the best works of art, though some of man's creations are very fine, too. Don't you think that's profound, I mean fantastically simple and true? He has stones down there, too, and pieces of rock from the mountains. He says a woman's body is the most profound creation of all. He says any woman who rejects sex is a sinner.'

'And any man?'

'Of course.' Dusty fastened the top button on my dress. 'I've always wanted an older sister.'

'No brothers?'

'Ugh-ugh. Daddy divorced ten years ago. I scarcely remember her. But I gather she was never at home anyway, a bitch. Say, why did you go to the States anyway?'

'To teach.' I stroked her hair.

'Golly! Where?'

'A school in Illinois where there was snow on the ground five months of the year and the kids gave me hell. The assignment was supposed to be for two years, but after four months I couldn't take any more. I arrived in New York days before the boat was due to sail. I stayed at a cheap West Side hotel and every day I'd walk down to the pier just hoping for a glimpse of the ship that would take me away. I'm probably unjust to America. I could love it. I loved 3rd Avenue on Sunday mornings, having a late brunch of salt-beef sandwich, and the little shop selling gear for safaris in Africa, and the Hungarian and Italian restaurants, which made me feel the city belonged to the rest of the world and not just to America. But it was so impersonal. I didn't know anyone. I didn't know anyone until I met Marcello, on the way home.'

'The States needs a special kind of giving of yourself, especially New York. You've got to be a sweet, desirable package. Money helps, of course. In New York I've had wonderful times, thanks to Daddy. Daddy will give me anything. Money, clothes, an American Express card and

60

any other you care to mention.'

'Such things help?'

'Well, being human, I do like luxury now and again. But basically, no. Daddy's a lawyer and filthy rich.'

'That's nice.'

'Not for Daddy. He's terrified. He doesn't talk about it of course, but I think he's mixed up with the Mafia.'

'You're joking!'

'One doesn't joke about the Mafia, believe me. And then he's terrified about me, thinking I'm maybe a chip off the old she-block, that I'm a nympho, just like mother. He's worried about my political activities, too, naturally. But he thinks those would cease with marriage. He'd like to see me married to a lawyer, of Italian descent, naturally, but not mixed up with *them*. He'd like to see me in a hundred thousand dollar house, with three kids, two cars, a TV in every room and membership of the best local country club. Hell! *That* man, daddy-style, but clean-all-American, gives me nightmares. I'm not going back to him!'

'And where does Daddy think you are now?'

'Up to a week ago, with the tour.'

'The tour?'

'Arranged by the school. "Five Culture Cities of Europe in Three Weeks." Madrid, Copenhagen, Amsterdam, Paris, Rome. Rome, as you can imagine, was the big attraction.'

'And where you quit?'

'Right.' Dusty laughed. 'I went out to Fiumicino by cab, not decided till the last moment. Would I join them for the return trip, or wouldn't I? They called me over the PA, and I just sat there in one of the bars, drinking Coke, and thinking, well, if they find me they find me and that's that, and it's Fate with a capital F for fuck everything. But they didn't, and the plane took off without me, and I took a cab back. Back to Marcello.'

'He was pleased to see you back?'

'He was surprised, eating spaghetti with his wife.'

'What did he say?'

'He said, "Well, I'll try and get you a room at the Pensione Fratelli, until you've sorted things out. Won't your father be worried?"'

'That was very paternal of him.'

'Well, you see, he has a daughter of his own. So he knows what it means. I mean to be worried about a daughter if one happens to have one. How did you get along with your father?'

'I didn't. He was a non-conformist clergyman with a strong sense of sin. He beat me. Most of the time, I lived in terror. But that's ancient history.'

'What happens in one's childhood is never ancient history. It's present and future.'

'One never grows up?'

'Maybe not. I'll have different opinions as the years go by.'

'You've met Marcello's daughter?'

'Fiametta? Ugh-ugh. She's spent the summer with her grandparents in the Dolomiti. She's due back in Rome soon. A reason why we'll have to leave. Another is that I expect my daddy here, almost any day. He misses his darling daughter, but of course he has Beryl.'

'Who's Beryl?'

'Beryl is his secretary, a bigger bitch, by all accounts, than dear Mama ever was. She looks like her, too. Big hips, black hair and a mouth that when she laughs, looks like a dollar sign, with teeth.'

'Why doesn't she marry him?'

'Well, for one thing, she's been gettting more out of him the way things are. Tiffany never had it so good. But now she's getting restive and Dada wants, naturally, to protect his investment. The end of love often leads to marriage, I'm told. Say, how come you never married?'

The moment of truth. The moment that, even now, sets a cold hand on my belly. The moment that started the crime going.

Did I look doom-ridden?

'Hey,' Dusty said, 'You're still with me?'

'Here and somewhere else.'

'Like where, for instance?'

'Up north.'

'The Artic Circle?'

'Not so far north.'

'The north of England?'

I groped for and found the silver frame.

'His name is Henry.'

Dusty examined the photograph with care. 'He's old,' she said, finally.

'Fortyish. Anything else?'

'He has a funny look about him, and I mean peculiar. Here's a guy who has something he isn't going to share with anyone. He's not bad-looking, though.'

'No. He's the man I'm supposed to marry.'

'Then what's stopping you?'

'It's not very definite.'

'And how long has it been going on?'

'Nearly eight years.'

'Eight? You're kidding!'

'No, I'm not. But it's the understood thing.'

'And you'd give up your independence for *him*? You're that desperate?'

'Men seem to shy away. He's the only one. I'm afraid of being lonely.'

'When? In your old age – which is at least thirty, forty years off? *He's* the monkey on your back?'

'Henry is an old and dear friend.'

'A bloody icon in a silver frame? You love him? I mean, he's supposed to be a man?' Dusty scrutinised the photograph again. 'He's not exactly bad looking.'

'No, he isn't.'

'And he reminds me of someone.'

63

'Oh really?'

'A friend of my father's. A guy named James who came over to our apartment one evening for some legal advice. Probably a criminal matter, since that's Dad's line of business. But Dad didn't show. He phoned, though, a few seconds after James had arrived. "Honey, is James there? He is? Then give him a drink and tell him I can't make it. I'll call him tomorrow. Be nice!" "Yes, Daddy!" Of course, he was busy with Beryl.

'James was an actor, a bit-part player till he was thirty-nine, and then suddenly he had the right face for a TV serial and he had become a big name and big money almost overnight. The nation's middle-aged heart-throb!

'And there he was, suddenly, in our living-room. I'd read all about him in the fan magazines. I knew what he weighed, what he ate for breakfast, also that, for no apparent reason, he'd take sudden swipes at people. For publicity, or for real? Does it matter? And he had another hobby, I'd heard; young flesh. Oh, course, people talk. But anyway, there I was, sixteen-years-old and all excited at the idea of playing hostess to a real-live movie, TV, what-have-you star.

' "Won't you have a drink?" I said, all girlish. "Dad said I was to offer you a drink."

'He flashed those famous teeth of his and said, "Why don't you call me James, and I'd very much like to have a drink."

'My hands were shaking as I picked up the gin bottle. It must have showed. "Here, better let me do that. Man's work," he said.

'So I went over to the phonograph and turned on some sweet, soft stuff, and then went over to the sofa and waited for him.

' "One for you."

'I'd never had a Martini before, but didn't like to admit it. So I simply took the glass and swallowed the stuff

64

quickly, to be rid of it as soon as possible. It must have been almost straight gin. I sat there, gasping, trying not to choke, James pretending not to notice. I stood up and, suddenly there we were, dancing. I closed my eyes and put my head on his shoulder and it was marvellous, not in the least like any of the proms I'd been to, not that what we were doing could be called dancing, anyway. After a while, he put another glass in my hand and said, "Hullo, Dusty!" and I said, "Hullo, James!" and drank more slowly this time so I wouldn't choke and feel silly and immature. And then we were dancing again, and not dancing. We were on the sofa and, boy, those kisses were like no others I've had before and my head swam with them and the Martinis, and he began feeling under my dress, which was something boys had tried with me at school before of course and I'd simply laughed, but this time I didn't laugh. I just lay there, shivering, though I wasn't the least bit cold, and there he was kneeling on the rug at my feet, and suddenly I was in a panic, jumping up and running to my bedroom and slamming the door, locking it and leaning against it, my hands against my cheeks so hot I might have had a fever.

'I could still hear the music, but after a little while it stopped and it was very quiet and I stood there, listening to nothing, thinking maybe he'd gone . . .

'Then I heard it, a very tiny sound, very close, a scratching on the door with his fingernail, and my shivering became worse and my teeth were chattering. I looked around the bedroom for some way of escape, but everything, though familiar, was a sort of blur, and then the scratching started again.

'I had a puppy once who scratched just like that when he wanted to come in, and I always *did* let him in because he was so soft and cuddly and I was sorry for him, and I cried and cried when he was killed by an auto out on the boulevard. And without consciously willing it, my fingers were turning the key . . .

'He had a funny look, a look I'd never seen on a man's face before. No, I don't mean funny. I mean sad, imploring, as if he were a little boy about to cry, and I rushed over to him and was in his arms, crying like a baby, pressing my mouth against his and my body against his, and he was picking me up and carrying me over to the bed ... I thought I was dying. I thought, if this is dying, I want death ... Afterwards, I began to be frightened, about what might happen, because I wasn't taking the pill then. Of course he said not to worry because if things went wrong he'd take care of me, and anyway, wouldn't I like to go into the movies because he could do a lot for a pretty little thing like me. Of course I told him I didn't expect anything like that, and had no talent anyway, and all I wanted, please, was that he should love me.

'It was getting late then, or early. Around four or five a.m., and I saw him glancing at the little clock beside the bed. I said not to worry because Dad would still be in Boston for sure and wouldn't be back for hours. Then he said he could use a drink and ambled into the living-room to fix one. He had one for me, too, when he came back, but I said, "I don't want a drink I want you." So we started again. It was coming light when he left the apartment.'

Dusty was still holding Henry's portrait.

'Appearances don't mean anything,' I said. 'Henry tried to make love to me just once. It was awful.'

Dusty looked at me thoughtfully, but made no comment. 'Anyway,' she said, 'I haven't finished the story.'

'Oh? There's an end?'

'You bet! Well, I half woke up and stretched out my hand, not opening my eyes, imagining James was still with me. Someone took it. Dad, looking at me in a very strange sort of embarrassed way. Was there some sign of James in the bedroom? Had I been talking in my sleep? There was of course also the usual explanation. Dad always looked embarrassed when he'd been spending the night with Beryl,

66

which he calls going to Boston. Beryl's apartment is just around the corner, and Dad pays the rent. Dad has been looking very worried lately and I think I know at least one of the reasons why. Beryl has been making all sorts of threats, including suicide, if he didn't marry her – I overheard her one night on the phone. But first he'd have to square it with me ... Anyway, there he was holding my hand and hiding something behind his back.

' "Hey, what have you got there?" I said. He nearly always brings me a present when he's been to Boston.

' "Sorry, honey, but this trip I didn't have a moment. Caught the plane by the skin of my teeth. But these are for you!"

'Gardenias! He bent down then and kissed my cheek. I couldn't very well throw my arms round his neck as I usually do because I was stark naked under the sheet.

'There was a card. *Thanks for a swell evening.* From James.

' "You must have been quite the accomplished little hostess," Dad said.

' "Oh, shucks! I didn't know what to talk to him about. He left early, probably bored to death."

' "Oh, what time was that?"

' "Around six, I guess." I didn't specify p.m. or a.m.

'Dad tried to look reassured, but he was probably thinking what a good liar I was turning out to be and that if I'd been a boy he would have sent me to law-school.

' "I'll have to call and thank him," I said.

' "Oh, I don't think I'd do that."

' "But why not? One must be polite."

'Actually, of course, I simply wanted to hear his voice and fix the next meeting.

'I must have looked pretty determined because Dad said, "Well, if you must, you must." He went out looking upset and unhappy.

'The second the door closed, I picked up the bedside

phone. A woman's voice answered. I said, "Hullo, please may I speak to James." She started screaming as if she was drunk.

' "You're one of his little playmates? You've a nerve, calling him at home. You think he's good and kind and handsome? Well, I tell you, he's a louse. He promised to open the studio door, the kingdom of heaven? The only door he ever opened for himself, without my assistance, was the door of the john! Or perhaps you think he's good in bed? Well, he should be. He's had enough practice, but not in mine. Hey, hey, maybe you're the kid he spent last night with, you little whore, you! You're calling to collect? Don't you imagine maybe he has a wife and family ... ? Hey, hey, you free-wheeling tramp you ...'

'I hung up.

'A little later, Dad came in, more worried than ever. Maybe he'd picked up the other phone in the living-room and heard everything. I'm not sure.

'But he said, "Honey, how would you like a trip?"

' "Like where, for instance?"

' "Europe."

'Thinking that I'd probably never see James again, and didn't want to, gave the idea a certain appeal. I felt awful, dirty, but still in need of more sex, if you know what I mean?'

'Yes,' I said.

'So I said, "Yes, please, Daddy, I'd like a trip to Europe just fine."

' "Escorted," he said. "Something cultural. How does that sound?"

' "Fine, fine!"

'Of course he wanted to sort Beryl out, without me around. And probably get me away from James.

' "You could leave next week."

' "I'd rather wait till summer and finish my studies."

' "You can catch up on those."

68

' "But why make life difficult?" '

' "Wouldn't it be more exciting to make a sudden decision?" '

' "But I like my work." '

'The argument went on – for weeks. Then I met Marcello, and stopped struggling. It was Europe, here I come! You know something? I bet he's got Beryl in the apartment by now. For reasons of economy. Boy, I bet she's costing him plenty! The other day I got a letter, from Daddy. Imagine! Usually he has no time to write. A letter filled with local gossip. Item: James' wife is dead. Of stomach poisoning! You suppose he could still use a good lawyer?'

'You mean he killed her? He's capable of such a thing?'

'Well, I suppose a man can stand only so much. I mean, everyone has a breaking-point. She was making his life a misery. Compare her with Clara, Marcello's wife, someone who truly understands a man. A woman like that has no right to live.'

'She was probably very unhappy.'

'So? So she was unhappy? Putting her out of her misery was doing her a favour. If she killed herself, so much the better.'

Dusty picked up Henry's photograph again and removed it from its silver frame. She handed me the $50.

'People who torture other people for their own pleasure,' she said, 'have no right to live.'

'Such people may be sick.'

'That doesn't give them the right to ruin the lives of other people.'

Very deliberately, Dusty tore Henry's photograph, first into two pieces, then into four, then eight. 'There,' she said, 'that disposes of Henry.'

I was angry, I confess. A perfectly good, even treasured, photo, ruined. 'Not exactly,' I said. 'To me Henry is still very much alive.'

'Because you need him?'

'Because I suppose he needs me as much as I need him.'

'Oh, stuff!' she said. 'Sentimental nonsense!' And suddenly she held her hands before my face.

They were small, but boney and competent, the fingers broad, spatular. I turned her left hand over and looked at the palm, examined the lines of fate, terrifying myself, though palmistry, I tell myself, is an insult to my intelligence.

'Well,' she said, 'what's the verdict?'

'You are good at games,' I said, not because I had come to that conclusion, merely needing something to say.

'Games? A word implying enjoyment, frivolity?'

'Perhaps.'

'To be worth playing at all, a game must be played with intent to win. Enjoyment is permissible, even desirable. But one must be fundamentally serious. Work can be a game. Also life – and death.'

Suddenly, I felt cold. 'Death, a game?'

'A subject with which I am very familiar. You know what subject I studied at school?'

'Biology, I think you said. The science of life.'

'Life always implies death. And renewal. Death implies violence. You are surprised I talk this way?'

'Yes, a little.'

'Because of my kissable mouth, my shapely bottom? Because I was the sweetheart of Sigma Chi? Simply because I'm a girl? Don't let such things fool you. Anyone can become a killer.'

'I'm not quite with you,' I said.

'A rat,' Dusty said, 'is to me, and to most people I guess, a loathesome animal. A rat is a rat. Detestable, obscene. But when I was first asked to kill one, in the lab, for dissection purposes, I couldn't do it. Not at first. There are two ways of killing a rat in the lab. You can either stick the animal into a box and chloroform it, the sissy way; or

70

simply bang its head against the bench, and it's dead in a jiffy.'

'And which method did you use?'

'Within a week I was knocking the rats' heads against the bench for pleasure. And down at Dad's farm in Maine, came the next vacation, I was wringing the necks of chickens without turning a hair. Now look at my hands again.'

They still seemed innocent, childlike, smelling not of dying flesh but cologne. 'I think you've a very fertile imagination,' I said.

A little later, she said, 'D'you mind if I talk about your case – I mean you and Henry – with Marcello.'

'Marcello already knows quite a lot about me and Henry,' I said.

I was still holding the $50 bill, feeling as if she had made me a present of it.

Six

Finding a plot has always been a little difficult. A 'story', anyway, was something I rather despised. My novels usually start with a place, a mood, a few characters whom I use to explore my own ideas, my attitudes, my sensations – and those, of course, of my friends, enemies and acquaintances. They meander on and, after perhaps some small changes have occurred in the relationships of the characters, they end, for no apparent reason, like life itself. I have fancied myself a latter-day Proust, concerned with time, with ennui (a common Italian preoccupation), with meetings and partings, with the incompatibility of men and woman. A beginning, a middle, an end? Till now, Aristotelian discipline has seemed too severe, or perhaps I am too lazy, too self-indulgent to accept the strictures of an organised plot. Just as my life has no well-defined pattern, no particular centre, no one woman. Moving from woman to woman, I sometimes imagine, knowing it is an illusion, that the one I briefly possess (who also possesses me) will provide me with a new beginning, a purpose other than literary. My vanity tells me I am bringing a brief, but valid, happiness (and longer, but equally valid grief) to my latest victim. My professional sense tells me that I am merely exercising my God-given right to collect material for my next book, or even the one on which I happen to be currently engaged, as, in my plotless stories, there is always room for a new character to liven things up.

The truth is that, like most novelists, I am a psychological ponce, living off my friends, enemies and women (who can be either); actually obtaining money from them, though indirectly of course, via my publisher, Caesare.

And of course there is my wife, Clara, who comes into a somewhat different category.

Three years ago, she was not only my wife but my enemy. We were about to part, a treaty arrived at after a long war.

But suddenly, almost overnight, she became my friend, my collaborator. I am still mystified. My mystification, for the moment, binds me to her. (She will provide new material for my next book?)

Except of course during my long absences, usually in America, we have always slept together, literally and sexually, the latter sufficiently often for me to feel that she was receiving her wifely due. No fire, merely a supine acceptance of, as it were, a right.

And then, suddenly, on my last return from the United States, it happened. The excellent housekeeper, the good cook, the acceptable wife (she has her own money, inherited and from her professional activities), became an ardent mistress.

A doctor, was she using some new drug that worked miraculously on her glandular system? Or was it that, after a three months' absence, she was simply hungry for a man, any man? My daughter Fiametta, aged sixteen, would simply look at us and say, 'It's ridiculous! Two middle-aged, married people, suddenly in love!'

Ridiculous, yes. But not true. It was simply that I was 'interested' in my wife again, intrigued by her, as a woman. Why was she suddenly involved with me, as a person, as a writer? Can *she* be a manipulator? That gentle, almost saintly creature! Is it possible?

The change in my wife, as I say, was apparent immediately on my return from my last visit to the United States. For several years now, it has been my habit, my pleasure and my pain to plunge, preferably in the winter, into the States, meaning, for me, New York. My wondering friends ask, why not Sicilia, why not Tunis, the Lebanon? And I

73

have to explain, patiently, that I must, now and then, descend into hell, which is what to me New York represents.

I say this in no derogatory sense. Hell is necessary, a part, a major part, of life, more essential than heaven – to a creative person, far more stimulating. Anyway, New York, appeals to the satanic in my nature, I fit in there, playing, an exotic middle-aged exotic, my successful and oft-repeated role of psycho-sexual gymnast. I plunge into those dangerous canyons, becoming involved with the perverse, the impure, the damned (as I like to imagine) of every race, colour and description. I draw upon the weed. I seduce and am seduced, and then, at the first hint of spring, when an improbable rebirth seems imminent, I return to Italy, to Rome, and also to my small white house beside the ancient sea, to brood about things seen and imagined.

But no matter how often I return, how familiar it becomes, I am unable to write about the city. Hell, as a writer, eludes me. Certainly, I have tried to capture it, but always I am dissatisfied with the result. Possibly this is because, in spite of my near-perfect English, I can only write in Italian. As a writer – the Italian public is necessarily limited – this disturbs me. (American-Italian contacts seem to be more significant on a culinary, business, military and criminal plane rather than the cultural.) There is also the financial consideration.

To explain. Since my marriage, I have always been more or less financially dependent on my wife. She has a profession that pays a regular salary. I do not. She inherited money. I did not. For many years, this did not disturb me particularly. I was, after all, a poet, an artist. And who better a patron, disinterested, purely loving, than one's wife? Still, as Clara's inheritance dwindled, because of our rather extravagant way of life and the declining value of the lira, money became a problem. My male ego was affronted as I became increasingly dependent upon my wife's earnings.

74

My books sold, it is true, but only in Italy to a small number of the discerning, and I became aware that writing of my particular style was becoming increasingly unfashionable. In spite of my frequent contacts with 'America', I was no longer 'with it'.

When my latest little American, Dusty, and my peculiar English Miss Edwardes had been in Rome for a few days, I became rather bored, as usual, with the purely female complications, and longed to escape, if only for a few hours. Also, my wife had been so demanding, sexually, that, taking Dusty's demands also into consideration, it was essential to take a little time off.

A trip to Milan seemed a good idea, on both sexual and professional grounds. My latest novel, in my usual style, had been with my publisher, Caesare, for several weeks without even a note to say that the script had been received. I was worried.

So I drove the somewhat battered Alfa up the Autostrada del Sole, checked into the Elite (cheap hotels depress me, and anyway, Clara was paying), and phoned Caesare, saying I 'happened' to be in Milan, and what about lunch?

'I'm not eating lunch these days, my dear fellow,' he said. 'But I can give you half an hour, say, around twelve-thirty?'

I had not seen him for more than a year. His office was unrecognisable. Instead of being a place of agreeable literary disorder, it was now furnished as if it were the anteroom of a museum displaying the kind of canvas which consists of a single black dot on an immense white ground. Exotic plants flourished in the newly air-conditioned atmosphere, almost silent electric typewriters whirred, telephones glowed in a subtle harmony of ad-man's colour.

Wearing a superbly cut mohair suit (undoubtedly Savile Row), Caesare, my old friend, rose to greet me, I thought, with something less than his usual cordiality. He had lost many pounds; like his office, he was scarcely recognisable.

75

Even his manner was different. No longer effusive, volatile, even emotional, his manner instantly reminded me of that of some of the American executives in publishing and films with whom I had made unsuccessful and abortive contact during my descents into 'hell'. (I have always justified my visits to New York to my wife as being professionally necessary, and she usually contributes handsomely to expenses.)

The new style of management. Capitalism with a scarcely recognisable human face! (Like too many Italian intellectuals, I have toyed with the many faces of Socialism and Communism and found nothing but myself, seen in a mirror!)

I looked around this unreal, stage-set office. Autographed photographs of 'his' authors had graced the walls on my last visit, my own among them. Now nothing but virginal whiteness.

The secretary deftly removing the tape on to which he was recording as I entered, was no longer the middle-aged, friendly and fussy woman I had known for years, but a slim-as-a-reed, ice-cool blonde of the type I have often observed eating lunch-time salads in the coffee shops of Third Avenue. (In bed, however, I have found them as efficient and mechanical as the offices in which they worked.)

Lunch, in the old days, would have meant two hours at Savini's, to our mutual gastronomic delight. Now, at some unheard signal, a white-coated woman entered, with sandwiches on a tray, and glasses of milk.

'You'll join me?'

I winced. (I had, actually, rather been looking forward to a good lunch, at his expense – even mine!) 'Milk? Thank you, no.'

Caesare rose, moved to a refrigerated bar concealed behind a meaningless modern painting on the white bookless wall and mixed a negroni.

The result, I must confess, showed that he had not lost

76

his once famous skill.

'You will forgive me if I don't join *you*,' he said, 'but I have a conference in a half-an-hour.' He glanced at his watch to convince me of the value of his time.

'Time is important, Caesare?' I said, remembering the old days.

'Times change,' he said. 'In Italy, especially in Milan. Even in Rome.'

'Meaning one particular Roman citizen? Me?'

'Perhaps.'

'About the book?' I said.

I had noticed the typescript of my novel on his desk.

Caesare drew a deep, regretful breath. 'Marcello,' he said, 'I am truly sorry, but against all my pleadings, my colleagues have decided that your novel does not fit into our particular programme at present.'

He was lying, of course, Caesare did not have colleagues. He had employees, people who obeyed his orders. He leafed through the typescript, as if recalling to mind its contents.

'A work of great sensitivity,' he said, 'beautifully written, containing many, many fine things. The work of a true poet. But alas for poetry!' He glanced at a memo-pad (evidently he had had himself well-briefed for my visit). 'Your last book, dear friend, sold three thousand, three hundred and four copies. Over a period of two years! Production costs were not covered.' He sighed. 'You are thinking, perhaps, that our dictionaries, textbooks, works of non-fiction, best-selling novels, should subsidise more poetical works that sell only to the discerning few? But today this is a business, like any other. A book is a commodity, a product, which must be in demand. Or for which a demand can, by astute promotion, be created. Publishing is a business in which all the techniques of modern management can, and must, be applied.'

'The Bible has been quite a good seller for a number of years, without modern management techniques,' I said.

77

'Not to mention Tolstoy, Dickens, Maupassant, who wouldn't even know what you are talking about.'

'True. But they produced the right product. By flair, instinct, talent. But we live in a super-market age. And the writer, like any other producer of merchandise, must move with the times, or go under.' He looked at me appraisingly. 'Some of the most successful novels today have been manufactured. Assembled, if you like. To the profit of the author and publisher alike.'

Caesare's eyes glittered. I recalled that he had recently acquired a villa on the Costa s'Emerelda, a five-ton motor cruiser and, it was rumoured, a new mistress (he was long and miserably married).

'Have you ever considered,' he inquired softly, 'writing a faction?'

I raised my eyebrows. 'A what?'

'A work combining fact with fiction, designed to provide the ever-growing reading public with both instruction and entertainment. The fact, of course, must be exciting, connected with some great modern enterprise. Aviation, for example, or the petroleum industry. The fiction must be sensational, erotic, even pornographic. There are passages in your last book which suggest you could carry off the sex parts of such a book very successfully.'

'Thank you.'

'But unfortunately the passages come at infrequent intervals. My reader (he glanced again at his memo-pad) 'counted a mere five brief "purple-passages", if you permit the phrase, in a typescript of over three hundred pages!'

I hung my head. In shame for myself, or him?

Caesare indicated a cigarette-box which incorporated also a clock and a small radio.

'Tobacco,' he murmured, 'is alas a luxury I no longer permit myself.'

On my last visit to Milan, not so very long ago, he had been a forty-a-day man with a cough to prove it, and a

78

crumpled suit encrusted with tobacco ash.

I inhaled deeply.

'You are angry?' he asked.

'Of course not. I find what you say profoundly interesting.'

'Good. Listen, Marcello, old friend, I have been talking of business, but that does not mean I am without sentiment. I would like to help you, if humanly possible. If you are short of money . . .'

'I am a writer,' I said, 'to most writers shortage of money is endemic. We accept it, regretfully, as a fact of life.'

'But you feel frustrated, defeated, finished? Like a man who can no longer make love even to his wife?'

'I have no problems in that connection,' I said.

'Oh, really?' He seemed surprised. 'But to you women never were a problem. I know you moved from one to another seeking inspiration. But don't you think it time you found another source?'

'Than women?'

'Yes.'

'You're implying I'm getting old?'

'None of us is getting younger. But is sex enough? People are getting their kicks now in many other ways.'

'Of course. But I don't know anything about industry, or science.'

'There is such a thing as research.'

'You're suggesting I should work in a factory or something? Never!'

'Research,' he said, 'often simply consists of picking someone else's brains.'

'My work,' I said, 'has always been original, owing nothing to anyone but myself!'

'Marcello,' he said, wagging a finger, 'you have put your friends and enemies into all your books. I have recognised myself. I did not know whether to be flattered or annoyed. I am a frustrated novelist. I know your problems. But you

79

have to face the fact that all writing, yes, even creative writing, is research – into one's self and others.'

'You are leading up to something,' I said. 'Why not come out with it?'

'I was trying to help you,' he said, looking pained, 'as a writer. But if you wish me to be direct, so be it. Listen.' His voice was suddenly conspiratorial. 'The other day a young engineer came to my office. He had just returned from one of the Trucial States – a sheikdom – where he has been, and still is, involved with some kind of construction work to do with oil. He came to Milan to visit his sick father, who has just died.'

'Then why did he come to see you?'

'Because he has literary ambitions.'

Caesare was now looking exceedingly crafty.

'Go on,' I said.

'He cannot write.'

'He is illiterate?'

'I mean he writes like an engineer. His manuscript . . .'

'Ah, he submitted a manuscript?'

'Of course. It reads like some kind of technical report, all facts, figures, data. But . . .' Caesare reached into a drawer of his enormous desk and produced a bulky script. 'But, buried in this unpalatable, unseasoned pasta of a book, there are astonishing and authentic facts. The private life of the sheik . . . the young engineer has access to the palace; I think he must be homosexual. The strange habits and morals of the sheik's European and American military, economic and political advisors. The sheikdom, you understand, is undergoing development on an unprecedented scale. There are Russian, Israeli and Egyptian spies. There is even a British film company that went out to make a documentary about the construction work, but produced a blue movie for the sheik's delectation instead! My dear Marcello, in this dark, almost impenetrable mine, there are the makings of a bestseller. A book that would take all

Europe, America, England, the world, by storm! Think of the paperback rights, the serial rights, the film rights! All that is necessary is that you dig for the diamonds, polish them, add the literary lustre that is peculiarly your own. Without, of course, the lengthy psychological probings you too often indulge in.'

I was interested, I confess.

'All right,' I said, 'where can I meet this engineer?' I took an old envelope and pencil from my pocket. 'What's his address?'

Caesare took a sip of milk and a bite at his chicken sandwich.

'A meeting is not really necessary.'

'But how on earth can I pick his brains if . . .'

'The material is all here.' He tapped the typescript with a fastidiously manicured finger. 'He is a very ordinary young man. I think, as I said, he is a homosexual. He would bore you.'

'Perhaps I could draw him out.'

'His father's funeral is tomorrow.'

'Still, perhaps before he returns to the Middle East . . . ?'

'He is leaving the day after tomorrow.'

I began to get the picture. Caesare had made me squirm. Now it was his turn.

'And presumably he expects the return of his manuscript before his departure?'

'Just so. With my sincere regrets. However, that needn't worry us.'

Caesare walked to his wall-safe, opened it and handed me a Xeroxed copy of the typescript.

'Perhaps, dear friend,' I said, 'I should write a faction about aspects of the publishing business. I wouldn't have to do much research.'

'Author eats publisher? A kind of cannibalism. Quite unthinkable.'

'A joke is a joke.'

'How true.'

'But seriously,' I said, still intrigued in spite of my moral scruples, 'you can't expect me to write about a country, a part of the world, I have never visited. I have to experience the heat, the food, the flies, the women.'

'Heat, flies, food, women you know about.'

'Still, the burning, on-the-spot experience! Two or three weeks, a month at most!' The idea of getting away from Italy at that particular moment was irresistibly appealing. But, as usual, I was short of cash. 'A reasonable thirty dollars a day,' I pleaded. 'A mere thousand dollars in all.'

Caesare's expression suddenly lost its unbounded optimism.

'Say, six hundred thousand lire.' A substantial concession.

Caesare stared with immense concentration at the abstract painting on the wall opposite his desk. He rose and examined the brush-work as if he had discovered in it, at that precise moment, some new and extraordinary meaning.

Was I there? Did I exist?

I said, 'If you have such confidence in this Middle Eastern faction and my ability to write it, six hundred thousand lire would represent only a trifling fraction of the profits.'

Caesare was staring into the middle distance. Then, quite suddenly, he became aware of my presence.

'A remarkable work,' he said, presumably meaning the painting. 'That block dot. A master-stroke!'

'Six hundred thousand, Caesare,' I reminded him, knowing of course that he had not the slightest intention of giving me a single lira.

'My dear fellow, you know it has never been the policy...'

'Of your firm to commission novels. Yes, I know. But as you were speaking about the novel as some kind of manufactured product, the publisher, as manufacturer, should

82

obviously put something, make an investment, into basic research?'

'And dictate what you, the author, the creative person, should write? We aren't all Communists in Italy yet!'

Suddenly, in one of my flashes of insight, I knew that Caesare wasn't talking about writing at all. He was my enemy. He was jealous of me. But why? What had I got that he could possibly want? In some obscure way, was he trying to buy me off?

I was angry. But also excited, as, with me, is always the case when I feel some new literary idea stirring. An idea that was quite unconnected with our, to me, ridiculous conversation.

'Let me see your next script,' he was saying, gently propelling me towards the door. 'But make it contemporary. *Now!* Readers simply aren't interested in the hang-ups of the leisured intelligentzia any more.'

'Now?' I said. 'Such as a crime, happening next week?'

'I don't follow.'

'Caesare,' I said, 'there have been works of fact that read like fiction. Accounts of crimes based on the criminals' own words, describing their hopes, fears, emotions. Some of these books have been immensely successful.'

'True.'

'But suppose the author himself were to instigate the crime, and also persuade the criminal or criminals to make a record of the crime as it actually happened?'

Caesare looked at me, slightly amused. 'An intriguing idea, certainly. But first you would have to gain the confidence of some criminal or criminals ready, willing and able to commit the crime.'

'I wasn't thinking of working with ordinary criminals.'

'Oh really?'

'Ordinary people, admittedly under unusual circumstances, can be persuaded to commit even murder.'

We stood at the doorway. In or out? That was the question. I had his attention. Undoubtedly.

'You are thinking of some political assassination?'

'Political assassinations have been written about *ad nauseam*. Today, political violence is instant, in the newspapers. On TV. I was thinking of something more subtle.'

'The writer as murderer by proxy, crime as a literary exercise?'

'But fact not fiction. Such a book could, I think, be highly commercial.'

'It would have to do with some woman, or women, you know?' Caesare was, of course, aware of my bizarre way of life, my periodic descents into hell.

'Of course.'

I had suddenly the distinct impression that Caesare was frightened. 'Then perhaps I ought to hear no more about it.'

'You wouldn't be involved, except as publisher, and no publisher of the memoirs even of a war criminal, with millions of deaths on his conscience, has yet, to my knowledge, suffered, financially or otherwise. You would be simply producing a document of sociological interest, performing a public, if lucrative, service.'

'And you?'

'The dispassionate observer, recorder, editor. Doesn't the modern world make hypocrites of us all?'

'Expenses?' he asked, cagily.

'Work on this particular book would not involve my leaving Rome.'

'Very well. I would like to see the complete script.'

'In about two or three weeks.'

'So soon?'

'Until I came to see you today,' I said, 'I had not realised how far the act of creation had really gone.'

'Marcello, old friend,' he said, 'it seems absurd, but a writer should not, perhaps, get himself too deeply involved with life. You *know* what you are doing?'

'I am excited, not bored. That is enough.'

'I will publish your last novel, in spite of an almost certain loss.'

'My next faction will make a profit.'

So Caesare became my reluctant, anonymous confederate. I returned to Rome that same day, pressing the Alfa down the Autostrada del Sole as if my life depended on the exact moment of my arrival, which was, of course, anti-climax.

My flat was empty. Even Clara was out, at the clinic, presumably. There had been no need to hurry.

But later, around midnight, my crazy little American and my even more peculiar Englishwoman, came round, drank my wine and talked.

I had the concealed tape-recorder going. Now, their every utterance, no matter how trivial, seemed of breathtaking interest.

Miss Edwardes, when a little drunk, is very expressive. What she says could be printed, almost verbatim. *And* what she writes. Very little editing will be necessary.

The thing now is to speed them on their way, to get the crime going. (My little American is enthusiastic.) Also, of course, I do not want them here in Rome when my daughter returns from the Dolomiti. (Such old-fashioned scruples! I am ashamed.)

I shall miss Dusty, a charming, devoted instrument. Tonight, she talked about her father, a man, evidently, of influence. A man of Sicilian origins.

Can I use her and him, afterwards? ... I hear Clara coming from the kitchen, to tell me, no doubt, that the *saltim-bocca* is ready ...

Seven

Marcello,

You disappeared! For several days. To Milan, you said. Even after you returned, apart from that midnight chat, when we did meet it was usually for lunch at the cheap little trattoria in the piazza festooned with laundry and crucified shirts, and you were always surrounded with friends, the conversation mostly in Italian, with a word or two now and then in English, for my benefit. Crumbs to the undeserving foreigner. No hint at the renewal of any intimacies. I wasn't angry. Merely piqued. But now and then you did look at me in an oddly speculative way, and you asked to see what I had been writing. When I asked what you thought about my literary efforts you merely said they were 'interesting' – and that I should continue.

You were working hard, you said, on your new book. Also you were obsessed, understandably, with our little American. Me, too, Marcello. Me, too! It was to her unpredictable reappearances that I looked forward. Not yours. It was enough for me to know that you were in the same city, that I was writing, as it were, for you.

In those days, pleasant things would happen. Emerging from my deepest sleep at the *pensione*, half awake, I would have the feeling that she had slipped into bed beside me, unfresh from you, or perhaps some other man. But I wasn't angry, but welcoming. I imagined her as some little rejected animal, needing physical contact, human warmth. Involvement.

I was aware of course that she was 'political', but her interest seemed to be waning. Because of the heat? As the thermometer rose, the demonstrations and riots became less frequent, less violent. It was simply too hot to fight, to march, to shout.

It was a time to spend in bedrooms, shuttered against the heat. *My* room.

Marcello, I wondered if you would be jealous if you could see us as we sometimes lay there in that dim room, naked, talking. But it seemed so innocent.

One afternoon, Dusty said, 'He is concerned about you. But very busy. He says I should look after you.'

'I'd like that. Will you?'

'Of course. Let's go shopping.'

So shopping we often went as the city reawakened after the siesta, and my transformation from unswinging English teacher into hip cosmopolitan (at least as far as external appearances were concerned) proceeded at breathtaking pace. In the boutiques around the Via Condotti, under Dusty's guidance (and sometimes with her cash), I acquired a completely new wardrobe. It was Dusty who rearranged my hair, my face, even my body, because even my walk, the way I held myself, became different.

The teacher became avid pupil, and you, Marcello, like a benevolent guru, watched my progress from a distance.

Perhaps I should have felt humiliated by these attentions from my teenage mentor. But I did not. I felt flattered, as perhaps an unknown actress is flattered when she is being groomed for a part in a play unread, and perhaps even unwritten, but whose author has managed to convince his producers that he has conceived a work of staggering significance.

Farce or tragedy? I did not care. Only that I had got the part. I knew that your purely physical curiosity in me had been satisfied that last night as we sailed towards Naples, but that now you were possessed by a curiosity of a more subtle kind.

The steamy days and even steamier nights, when I lay

alone and uncovered, seeking sleep in imaginary mountains where the air was cool and fresh, seemed to merge into a shimmering haze of timelessness. I seemed inextricably involved in a way of life, indolent and almost mindless – apart from my writing which, anyway, seemed almost automatic – that would last forever.

Then one morning, when only the calendar told me I had been in Rome for just over seven weeks, I woke to find Dusty beside me. She was asleep. Her lips parted, features relaxed from those of young woman to those of an absurdly innocent child, wide awake, she was looking at me intently and, as I imagined at the time, with love.

I stretched out my hand and touched her hair. She kissed the tips of my fingers, then my ear, and whispered, 'It's seven-thirty.'

I stared at her. Usually we never even thought of getting up before ten.

'Time to go.'

'Go?' I echoed stupidly.

'Away from here. Away from Rome.' She placed a finger on my lips to prevent further questions. 'Come. I'll start the shower.' The room was in semi-darkness.

By this time, as of course you will understand, Marcello, I was accustomed to obedience. Obediently I got up; obediently I stood under the shower. Dusty busied herself with making instant coffee on the little portable stove we had in the room.

I had been late to sleep, reading half the night, vainly awaiting her return. Still numb from the icy shower, shivering in the bathrobe, then, sipping the coffee, I became aware that the homely disorder with which I usually surrounded myself – clothes, books, newspapers everywhere – had vanished. I was in a hotel room again, tidy and depersonalised; a non-room, no longer belonging to me.

My bag was packed, but still open. On top of my neatly

folded clothes was the silver frame that had once contained Henry.

Panic, almost terror. Yes. But almost a kind of pleasure in handing oneself over completely to the will of another. Once, when in hospital, undergong a minor operation with only a local anaesthetic, the sensation, in abandoning oneself to the surgeon and his aides, had been almost exactly similar.

Dusty handed me the clothes she expected me to wear.

'The cab will be here in ten minutes. Drink your coffee.'

'Cab?'

'To Fiumicino.'

'We're flying? But where?'

She was putting the finishing touches to her own sparse make-up. 'Into the past, and the future.'

'Science fiction?'

'A bit of both. Science and fiction.'

'But why the rush?'

'Well, for one thing, I'm trying to keep one jump ahead of Daddy. He's planning a European tour, with Beryl. I think she hooked him, I think they're married.'

Our destination was, in fact, Britain. I had been away less than a month. It felt like centuries. My home, that chintzy cell of female loneliness, with its wee dollies and teddy bears, its useless gadgetry in kitchen and bathroom, seemed, to the new me, as if we were entering the site of an archaeological dig where every footfall, the slightest unguarded movement could disturb and possibly destroy priceless evidence. We entered as if visitors from another world.

Dusty looked around my living-room with a kind of clinical interest.

'There!' she said, pointing, and from my suitcase produced the silver frame and placed it, with extraordinary accuracy on the mantelpiece, about a foot away from the clock that had once been my father's, now stopped, registering time past but not yet dead.

'A little to the left,' I said. 'About three inches.'

So Henry, imaginary, but framed, was briefly reinstated.

'An ikon,' Dusty said. 'A moment for lighted candles, for solemn music.'

She picked up the first record that happened to be lying on the top of the hi-fi. Vaughan Williams' *Fantasia on a Theme by Tallis*.

'This is solemn?'

'Very. It sounds best when played in a church.'

'At funerals?'

'Parts of it would be very suitable, if the estate of the deceased ran to the expense of a string orchestra.'

Dusty placed the record on the turntable and listened attentively as the sonorous mosaic of sound transformed my cosy living-room into a bare-walled, heaven-seeking chapel.

'Groovy,' she said, and pointed to the empty frame. 'You think *he'd* appreciate it?'

'He's not particularly musical.'

'What is he, particularly?'

'Nothing much.'

'We'll see. After all, one reason I came to England was to see Henry. It will be very amusing.'

I stared at her, astonished. 'To see Henry? You think he's some kind of joke?'

'If he is I'll laugh.' She glanced at her calendar watch. 'Today's Wednesday. Will you drop him a note and tell him to expect us on, say, Saturday?' She kissed me in that quick, impulsive way of hers. 'Cheer up,' she said. 'Me, I'm terribly tired. Would you be an angel and fix me an omelette and bring it up to me in bed?'

I was happy to oblige.

A small English seaside town was no place for Dusty. I tried to interest her in the local sights, the Gothic church, the Norman castle, the Roman remains, the antique shops, the old pubs – all the places that, over the years, had given me pleasure. She wasn't interested, and, extraordinarily restless, talking only of hitting the road, getting on the move.

So I took my old Morris to the garage, had new plugs fitted and an oil change, and I was ready. I had phoned Henry. Writing would have given him a chance to say he wasn't prepared for a visit at the moment. (And anyway, I had never been in the habit of simply dropping in on him – ours, as you will have gathered, wasn't that sort of relationship.)

But he seemed pleased by the idea, especially when I said I would, if he had no objection, be bringing a friend.

'An American?'

'Yes, very young and rather sweet. I'm sure you'll like her. She's a sort of pupil of mine.' I thought it diplomatic to lie a little.

'Fine,' he said. 'Mother's ill of course.'

'Oh well, in that case . . .'

'It makes no difference. You must come.'

He had never been so insistent before. For a second, I felt touched, then began to wonder. Did he want to see me, or Dusty?

'How ill is your mother?' I asked.

'She's dying,' he said, matter-of-factly. He was, I think, a little drunk. 'But don't let that deter you. The process could take quite a long time.'

We left the following evening, and suddenly Dusty seemed happier, being on the move.

'To be on the road and roll. That's what I like, what I like to do back home,' she said.

Eight

Amore mio,

Marcello, my lollipop! I long for you, I crave, I burn. But fifteen hundred miles away, I do your bidding. I hang on to our English miss as if my life depended on it, as, in a way, I suppose it does. I wish you were here, to discuss strategy – and of course for more personal reasons – but I'm acting according to the general *modus operandi* agreed.

I hope you will be pleased with me, but I am becoming a little suspicious of your motives, *cara mia*, in sending me away. You're really collecting material for a novel? Or simply getting rid of two females who might be an embarrassment if we were still around when your darling daughter returns to Rome?

I don't blame you, of course. I fully appreciate the problems of fathers who have unusual sex lives. And your daughter is almost exactly my age. But if anything happens to me, I'll haunt you! That's a warning! But with love and desire, ruining your sleep, and making you wish the ghost would become flesh. But, seriously, I think you are manipulating me with your oh-so-clever brain. Am I just a puppet? Perhaps the whole thing is simply a way of relieving your Roman boredom. You're doing it for kicks? It doesn't really matter. Perhaps I am also simply trying to fill the days. Drink tends to make me feel sick, suddenly; and pot I'm afraid of. Only your love-making makes me feel alive. Apart of course from conducting this little experiment you have devised . . .

I am encouraging her to talk of course, and to write, and she is dutifully writing down things as they occur to her (mostly in bed at night), and she will no doubt be sending her literary efforts to you for approval.

Of course she is obsessed with sex, and with me. I let her fondle me from time to time. Does that idea excite you? I am scribbling this very late at night, in an inn that was built in 1670 or something, after a horrid day. Miss E is asleep.

We left that depressing sea-side town at dusk, I with relief; but she seems to have a sentimental attachment to the place. I can understand why she went a bit nuts. You're naughty, *amore mio*. You should do your own research. Do I get a percentage of any financial rewards? Or, more interesting, a part of you?

Daddy will, I fear, arrive in Europe within a few days. There was a cable from him at American Express, London, which talked about 'we'. You can imagine what that means! Beryl! He may very well be on his honeymoon. I don't know which European city he will hit first, but my guess is London. I'll have to meet them of course, but by then I hope our little project will have been satisfactorily completed.

Unangelic *innamorato*, what have you been doing today? Screwing another little American, foreign, or even Roman, girl, and then telling your understanding wife all about it over the *saltimbocca*? And then did you screw *her*? She must adore you. Or has adoration given way to scientific curiosity and mere physical need, I mean for the kind of sexual fireworks you specialise in, you old pyro-technician, you. Loathsome, utterly revolting, totally beloved, you!

Say, perhaps I'll turn the tables and write the novel myself. Would you be furiously jealous? Or proud of me? Would it depend on who did the better job? You with your experience, or me with my 'innocence' and 'freshness'?

There! Doesn't that give you something to worry about?

Of course you can buy me off at any time, by taking me back to your bed, making me the supine companion of your typewriter. But we'll talk about this later. Just don't imagine you can make a fool of me, you gorgeous creature, you.

The point I'm making, *caro mio*, is that you mustn't imagine you can get rid of me easily, or at all. If I don't wish it.

But don't worry too much. Be kind, and I'm putty.

I'll be in touch, I hope, again soon. Love to Clara. I expect you will show her this letter anyway, and I want her to know how much I sincerely admire and respect her. And envy her, too! Sharing with you that enormous bed, *matrimoniale*. Henry, here we come! Dusty.

Nine

Henry Walton testing ... Henry Walton testing ... Well, the thing seems to be working all right, which pleases me no end. I'm very partial to gadgets, and have enough money to indulge. Mother encourages me, of course, as she encourages me in any expenditure, however unnecessary. But gadgets are my especial joy. Such as this small, neat Japanese cassette recorder I bought only the other day. I have gadgets of every conceivable kind, from an electrically heated seat for my personal WC to an electrically driven massager which is supposed to reduce my stomach bulge. The latter has not, as yet, produced dramatic results, not surprisingly, perhaps, in view of the amount of whisky I drink. Mother worries about my drinking, of course, but knows that if I cut it down I might turn to other more socially damaging pursuits. So she doesn't protest too much ... Henry Walton testing ...

Having just played back the foregoing, I must say I am quite pleased with the sound of my own voice. Ever since schooldays, I have been terrified of making any kind of public utterance, whether in public bar, private school or public meeting. At the crucial moment, my throat muscles would contract, my mouth would go dry, and my thoughts, such as they were, would become scrambled, so that when I opened my mouth the only sound that emerged was a titter-provoking, incomprehensible stutter. And yet my brain teems with ideas, fluently expressed in dream or when alone. Perhaps, though I really do not believe it, my problem is a dental one. I do not, I regret to say, have my soft-gummed mouth cared for sufficiently often, mostly because of fear of yet another gadget. The dentist's high-speed drill.

95

Oddly enough, on the rare occasions when I do visit the torture chamber, I actually enjoy myself. He, the dentist, has one of those newish chairs, fully reclining. To hand myself over, completely, has a certain pleasure. If I were not so terrified of pain, I would see him more often. This is another thing I cannot understand about myself: this reluctance to repeat an experience which is compounded equally of pleasure and fear . . .

Like everyone else, I suppose, I have this urge to express myself, to write, which is of course just another form of exhibitionism. What distinguishes the true writer, the professional, from the amateur, is, no doubt, the ability to transmute experience into something which is not simply personal, autobiographical.

No matter. I have no literary pretensions. I am simply amusing myself with a gadget which happens not to be a typewriter, but a tape-recorder.

Here I sit, in my own wing of the house, haunted, it's said, by the ghost of an eighteenth-century coachman who slept with my great-great-grandfather's wife and who was murdered, under peculiarly gruesome circumstances, for his pleasure. He is said to 'walk' every 3rd of September – five days from now. I have waited patiently for years, but so far haven't had the pleasure. A pity! I have always wanted to have intimate conversation with a man endowed, to put it crudely, with a cock and who is ready to use it.

There, limply, hangs my tragedy. I have tried everything, including books of a certain kind, under plain cover, sent from emporia in Soho, Copenhagen and Hamburg; and also certain devices from the same sources. But nothing seems to help. I have a hankering for the real thing: a woman, infinitely compliant, infinitely willing, who probably does not exist. And I confess that I get more pleasure, though of a different sort, from my collection of cigarette cards, started by my father (whom I scarcely remember) and to which I add, by regular deliveries, from a dealer in

96

London. Somehow, the cigarette cards, 'Struggles for Existence', 'Early Motor Cars', 'Uniforms of All Nations', etc., etc., give a continuity to my own existence, a meaning, a vague, but persistent search for identity...

Playing this back, it occurs to me that, if the narrative is to have any kind of sense, I must identify myself to the listener, in the manner, as it were, of the heroes of Victorian novels.

Very well! My name is Henry Walton and the great-great-grandfather I have already referred to, was one of those responsible for the English industrial revolution. By which I mean he built revolting cotton mills and row upon row of sordid dwellings (to give future slums a fancy name) to accommodate his slaves.

He also built himself, on the outskirts of the simple village which was soon to become an unlovely, 'where-there's-muck-there's-money', town, a house. This house.

A house? Rather a fortress to hide in, to make forages from in search of plunder; a castle to campaign from against the peasants who were attracted from the purple moors and the green fields, by the lure of money, which, like most lures, was an illusion.

Around this house, conceived in Victorian gothic, he built a high wall, and in the house he collected a huge accumulation of early Victorian furniture, silver, Sheffield plate, bric-a-brac, wine, port and whisky, and pictures, mostly of doubtful merit, as he was no latter-day Grand Tour connoisseur. My forebears seldom travelled. Lancashire was their world. My great-great-grandfather took some interest in the politics of India (whose people bought his finished cloth), and Egypt and America (who supplied the raw cotton). He would quarrel with the policies of politicians in a remote London. But there his wider interests ceased.

Still, the house is like a museum of an age, remote, even romantic now that the poverty and squalor are no longer so insistent on eye and nose and ear. A comfortable museum that is also my home ...

How confident and well-pitched my voice sounds now as I play-back, how easily the words flow. Or do I flatter myself? True, it is after 2 a.m. and I have consumed about a half-bottle of old Highland malt and so feel reasonably relaxed. When I talk to anyone other than this gadget, my voice is strained, rises in pitch ... Have I already said that? Drink helps. When I drink at the few social occasions I attend, I usually say something scandalous or insulting. Without meaning to, of course. The words simply slip out.

Where was I? Oh yes, I was introducing myself. So now, since she is the centre of my existence, I had better admit it at once: I am Mother's boy.

In a few days, I will be forty. She is well-turned seventy. Until two weeks ago, she sat in her part of the house, and I sat in mine. At dinner – breakfast and lunch I take in my own quarters – we would meet. Conversation was minimal; but always she watched my face. Searching for some sign of 'a cure'? Of my 'malady', as she chooses to call it, the original cause of my incarceration, if one discounts mother-love and the first prison of the womb itself, followed by the nursing arms, then the pram and after that the reluctant transfer to the comparative freedom of playpen and nursery.

I was, as they say, a delicate child. That is to say, I was subject to coughs and colds. I had stomach upsets which our doctor, an old fool, put down to a weak constitution when he should have recommended psychological treatment both for myself and my mother.

My father? Five years after I was born, he ran off with another woman and is now, if alive, somewhere in the United States, and I harbour no resentment whatever! I envy him.

Before leaving, he made all his honourable arrangements,

handing over the house and his income from the mill to Mother, who did not, of course, in the least appreciate his generosity, considering the hell she had made of his life here. I can still hear the shouting as I, myself unseen, a small, terrified boy wetting his pyjamas and thought to be asleep, saw her belabouring him with the pointed heel of her shoe. I remember the plaster on his face the following day when he said, patting my head, that he had cut himself shaving.

It was, I think, about a week after that incident that he disappeared.

His name has never been mentioned by my mother since. I have no idea how exactly he offended her. But just once, I remember vividly, when I was thirteen and she surprised me masturbating in the bathroom, she informed me I was going mad like my father. So I imagine their animosities were mainly sexual. Anyway, I was given to understand that sex was evil, or at the very least, indecent, and that I would come to a bad end.

Of course I have read every book I can lay hands on about sex, and I know that everything Mother said was total nonsense. Still, the feelings of guilt remain. When she gazed at me during dinner, often I felt she was remembering that particular scene.

Our dinners ceased two weeks ago, when she took to her bed and the nurses were called in. Since then, I have felt extraordinarily released, free. Should I feel guilty about this, too?

So! I went to a prep school for delicate boys, and after that to a school in the Welsh hills run by two food faddists who succeeded in under-nourishing both our bodies and our brains. The only decent meal we ever had was once when an Inspector arrived from the Ministry of Education; and on that same day, I remember, we also even had a few interesting lessons, on subjects ranging from Plato's *Republic* to the anatomy of the house-fly. The Inspector went away well pleased, and we pupils returned to our former state of mental and physical semi-starvation.

However, my health did improve, miraculously. Probably because we spent so much time in the open air. And then, as the prospectus said, games were encouraged, 'the pupil being free to select the sport of his choice.' This, for most, was of course solitary or group masturbation. Apart from this, few boys fancied football or cricket, or any team games, in fact. On one rare occasion when cricket was actually played, a pupil was struck by the ball with such force on the face that he had to be taken to the local hospital. I have never, to this day, seen so much blood. Cricket thereafter became a dirty word, the teams continued to exist only in name, and the boys continued to play chess, ping-pong and poker. One Scottish boy opted for tossing the caber, but a caber was difficult to come by and he started tossing dice instead. Though not really the gambling type, I actually won a few quid from him. Another boy took up rough shooting and put a few pellets in the behind of one of the masters he didn't care for, accidentally on purpose. I wonder how many of the old boys are, have been, or will end up in jail?

My own sport? For some extraordinary reason, I opted for golf.

Golf! I hadn't the slightest talent of course, but it was a good excuse to get right away from the school and have something decent to eat at the club-house. I had had a half-set of clubs for Christmas (which I still have, for sentimental reasons – though I've bought splendid full sets since), and took a few lessons from the professional. But he soon despaired – no muscle co-ordination – and I'd go off on the course by myself and bash away, playing hell with the greens. Being an unsociable type, I've never replaced a divot in my life.

But I enjoyed myself, not simply because the golf gave me freedom of a kind to enjoy the wind, the sun, the butterflies, the birds that soared over that small but remote course; but also because I was fascinated by the ballistics of the game.

Once, I actually did the short third, an 8-iron shot, in one. Fantastic, unbelievable! A fluke of course. But I have never felt such exhilaration since. But it was my finest hour, just as it must have been for the boy who hit the master in the bottom.

Anyway, golf made the school just supportable. Shortly after my seventeenth birthday, I was released – back into the charge of Mama. She did not know what to do with me as she was certain from the evidence of my bed-sheets and pyjamas, that I was still "disgusting". I wasn't good enough, of course, to try for a place at any higher seat of learning. I still stuttered, which she probably imagined to be a sign of incipient idiocy. I read a great deal, though; almost everything I could lay hands on. I asked for a record-player for my birthday, and listened for hour upon hour, often far into the night, to Beethoven and Stravinsky, pop and *musique concrete*. This further convinced Mother of my abnormality (also my father had been fond of music), and I was banished to separate quarters over the coach-house, which pleased me no end.

I mention all this merely to indicate that the cultural impulses are there! Somewhere in heart, brain or guts. But the headaches, the days of head-filled-with-dough feelings, persisted, became more frequent.

Mother's gaze at dinner became increasingly penetrating and concerned . . .

What was she to do with me? I can understand her problem perfectly. How to retain her hold on me, to protect me, wallowing in the pride of maternal possession, and yet to give me some semblance of freedom?

Actually, her course was clear. I should be 'groomed' for my rightful place, my throne. The big leather-covered chair at the head of the boardroom table at the mill. At that time,

Mama was titular head of the firm (and had been since my father departed in search of better things). But my uncle Charles actually ran things, as managing director.

Uncle Charles, who had a son of his own and who anyway, I felt, disliked me intensely, opposed the idea of my entering the mill and said I should take up music, professionally, instead. But Mother was, still is, a forceful woman. Uncle Charles was over-ridden and I was crammed, day and night, with facts and figures and the technicalities of the business, of which Mama had, I was surprised to discover, a remarkable knowledge. I was bored. I was harassed and nagged, and became even more bored and rebellious. I wanted to abdicate. Mother wouldn't hear of it.

Though the mill was less than a mile from the house, I had never actually entered it until I left school. Strangely remote, designed solely for the production of money, still it was magical on winter evenings when, ablaze with light, it seemed to float like a liner out at sea. As a child, I would imagine it moving splendidly out of sight, sliding past buoys and a headland, rising majestically to the challenge of the ocean. (How the words do pour out at 3 a.m., with the bottle three-quarters empty!) But of course the mill remained static, an immovable object, resisting all change, a monument to Victorian and my forebears' greed. It was doomed, though it seemed as immutable as an edifice of a vanishing religion. Inside, the spinning frames in ordered rows seemed to me to be altar-like, tended by virgins and non-virgins, administering some strange mechanical rite with flying fingers.

At first the humid atmosphere was almost suffocating, and there was the smell, compounded of cotton, oil and women. The smell of women who looked at me slyly, the young boss as I moved timidly among them. In that heat, they wore little more than thin dresses, also of cotton, and the sweat made the dresses cling to their bodies, and I was

102

almost sick with distaste, terror and desire. A few would smile, brazen, bold, inviting.

The first day I went among them, I remember, was a Friday. Many had their hair in curlers. Tomorrow, in Saturday finery, they would be ogling the men in the clubs and pubs and dance halls, pressing their bodies against the partners of the evening. And then? Copulating in doorways, in cars, even in beds? To my virginal mind, they represented a sort of primitive, untamed, man-eating femaleness, held in check only by their servitude to the machines. Suppose the machines stopped! Terrified, I hurried back to the safety of the office block, yet once there thought only of them, the blonde, perhaps, or the red-head, or the little Indian girl, wondering what it would be like to screw any of them or all. And I imagined them, prostrate and willing, spread-eagled across the boardroom table and me exercising my inalienable *droit de seigneur*. These fantasies filled my days. I had nothing, as merely heir apparent, to do. Sometimes, I would go to Nottingham, ostensibly to see the people who bought our yarn there, but actually to have a mostly liquid lunch at an old pub built into the castle rock, and feel that I had some part in history. And sometimes I would go to Manchester and listen to the jargon of the men in bowler hats on 'Change (now closed), and feel I had no part in anything.

But, on some excuse or other, I kept going back into the mill. There was one girl, in particular, a pretty dark little thing, about my own age . . .

One afternoon a week, if the weather was decent, I would tell the girl on the switch-board that I was going down to Manchester. In fact, I was going to the golf-course on the edge of the moor, busy enough at week-ends, but usually deserted other days. I had only the peewits and crows and the sheep for company, and I hooked and sliced away, glad to be free from the sexual assault of the mill and the unutterable boredom of the office.

Clever fellow! I was careful to arrive home at the usual time and meet Mother's scrutiny with what I hoped, briefly, was composure.

But there was no fooling her.

'You're flushed!' she would say. And of course my skin was still hot because of the sun and the exercise. She knew I had something to conceal. 'Something went wrong at the mill?'

Mother was always expecting plots against me and herself because of the animosity of Uncle Charles. She also imagined, with some justification, that he was ruining the business. True, the cotton trade was obviously dying, but Uncle Charles hadn't the imagination even to consider putting the mill to some other use. (The place, no longer owned by the family, is now devoted to the manufacture of plastic boats, and doing very nicely, thank you.)

Of course I always told Mother nothing was wrong and that Uncle and I had avoided each other, as usual.

Then came the awful day when I really had something to conceal.

We were eating our roast lamb and mint sauce and new potatoes and fresh peas when our maid, Hannah (the only person Mother is afraid of, because she is frightened of losing her) came in and said two strange men would like to see me.

'Men?' Mother said. 'What kind of men?'

'I don't know, they're not wearing uniform but they look like police to me,' Hannah said darkly. (She is an avid watcher of TV crime stories.)

'Did you take your car today?' Mother asked.

'Yes, but I didn't have an accident.'

'You're sure?'

'Positive.'

'Then what do they want with you?'

'I haven't the slightest idea,' I lied. 'Perhaps it's something to do with the mill.'

104

'Then they'd see you *at* the mill,' Mamma said, astute as always.

The detective inspector and the detective constable were waiting in the hall, the former a man with whom Mama was slightly acquainted. He addressed her with exaggerated respect since she was something of a mystery woman in the town, seldom seen, much talked about. (Of course everyone knew about Father.)

'This is a matter concerning your son, ma'am,' the inspector said. 'For the moment, I don't think we need bother you.'

'Anything that concerns my son concerns me,' Mama said. 'Why are you here? You'd better come into the living-room.'

The inspector looked very uncomfortable, sitting on the edge of his chair, and consulted his notebook.

'You were on the golf-course this afternoon, sir?'

Reluctantly, I agreed that I was, and Mama gave me a hard look.

'You are acquainted with a young woman by name Miss Elsie Pilkington?'

'I – I d-didn't know her name was Pilkington,' I stammered. 'M-mother, would you please go and finish your dinner?'

Mother ignored this request. 'What has my son had to do with Elsie Pilkington, Inspector?'

Somehow I had never supposed that detectives could blush. This one did.

'Well, ma'am,' he said, 'the young lady who is, I understand, employed at the mill, is making a certain accusation against your son.'

'Accusation? Please be more specific.'

'Well, ma'am, she is alleging rape.'

Mama did not look at me. She did not look at anyone.

She sat bolt-upright in her chair and said, 'Where did this – this incident happen?'

'On the golf course, ma'am, this afternoon.'

Still not looking at me, Mama said, 'Henry, will you please tell us exactly what happened?'

'I t-tried to make l-love to her.'

'Tried, sir?' the inspector said, gently, I imagined. 'The young lady claims that you violently attacked her, that you tore off parts of her clothing.' The voice became more neutral, as if he were giving evidence in court. 'This clothing has been examined by a police surgeon who has established that it has traces of semen. The surgeon has also examined the young lady, and he has found scratches and bruises on her body. What have you to say to that, sir?'

The constable waited, pencil touching paper.

'S-she's l-lying,' I said. 'I hardly touched her. I . . .'

'Yes, sir?'

'Well, if you must know,' it came with a rush, 'I – I e-ejaculated, that is the term, isn't it, before I even e-entered her.'

The constable's pencil was moving at considerable speed.

I went on, 'If her p . . . if her c-clothes were torn, s-she must have t-torn them herself, I mean, a-afterwards.'

'I see, sir. Then how do you explain the bruises on the young lady's thighs?'

'I – I c-can't explain them. Isn't there such a thing as s-self-inflicted injuries?'

My whole soul bared, I was shivering now, violently. I must have looked the very image of guilt.

'And the scratches, sir?'

'I s-saw her fall into a patch of brambles w-when she was running away.'

'Running away, sir? Why should the young lady run away unless she was afraid?'

'I – I imagine because s-she thought me r-ridiculous. She was laughing.'

'Laughing, sir?'

'Oh, d-definitely!'

'Would either of you gentlemen care for a coffee?' Mama said. 'Perhaps a brandy?'

'Thank you, no, ma'am,' the inspector said, answering for both of them. But he did accept a cigarette. The constable said he didn't smoke.

'So you deny the allegation, sir?'

'I – I do,' I said. 'E-emphatically!' I tried to put the sound of laughter into my voice, not very successfully. 'W-when it came to the point, I'm a-afraid I j-just wasn't u-up to it.' I giggled inanely.

'I see, sir.' The inspector was watching the constable's moving pencil.

'Pilkington?' Mama said. 'I know that family. A bad lot. The girl's father was once charged with causing malicious damage at the mill.'

'That may be so, ma'am, but it is hardly relevant to the matter in hand.'

'Charged, and found guilty!' Mama said. 'That, I think, is relevant, psychologically, if not in law. I gave orders that no member of that family was ever to be employed at the mill.'

'Then someone disobeyed your orders, ma'am.'

'Something,' Mama said, looking at me, 'that will not happen again.'

I don't know how she settled it, but I can guess. She probably paid cash to the Pilkingtons. I was off the hook.

Or rather I was swallowed and digested more completely by Mama than ever before. My 'shame' was scarcely mentioned. I didn't go to the mill any more. The house engulfed me. For months I took exercise only in the grounds. It was back to the womb . . .

The tape is running out, the bottle empty, the ashtray full. It is nearly 4 a.m. The background music is Brahms' Second Piano Concerto. (Is it true that he liked little girls,

107

so much easier to handle than full-grown women, I imagine?)

There was a call from her today, from Elizabeth. She is arriving tomorrow ... With a friend!

Ten

Marcello,

We are on the road, staying in an old inn, on the way to him, to Henry. We are occupying separate rooms, as it happens, so I can write to you without disturbing our little American.

I don't know why, but I have a compulsive need to tell you exactly how I first met him, and how I came to be his fiancee.

I met him in court. (Somehow a criminal background seems inescapable in my story.) Let me explain. I was home for the Christmas holiday, that is home from my teaching job on the south coast. Father was ill, but not ill enough for me to feel guilty about going to the New Year's Eve dance in the Town Hall. (He died three weeks later, unexpectedly and quite suddenly.)

As I had no escort, I went with a couple called the Hargreaves, and was deadly bored. Sam Hargreaves asked me to dance a couple of times, taking pity on me, no doubt. And then I was on my own. It was awful. I was thinking of calling for a taxi and going home, before midnight and celebrating the New Year solitarily in bed and, hopefully, asleep.

But it was only ten-thirty, and I decided to take a walk, inside the Town Hall. I walked down the long, broad staircase, and at the foot, pushed open a swing door. I was in court.

A single green-shaded lamp dimly illuminated the bench, the jury seats, the witness-stand, the lawyers' places, the dock itself. Everything seemed ready for some unknown drama. It was, I suppose, like being on a film set, at night. I realised I had been holding my breath, and I allowed the swing doors to close behind me.

It was suddenly very cold and I was glad I had brought my wrap. I was fascinated by the dock – a sort of enclosed platform on the same level as the bench. There was a door at the side through which the prisoner could be conducted to the witness-box to give evidence. But the real exit and entrance to the dock, I discovered, was not that way, but from below, down a flight of stairs leading to the police department and the cells.

Even now, on New Year's Eve, the police would be on duty down there, and in the cells there would be prisoners awaiting trial tomorrow. Happy New Year!

I stood in the dock, hands on the rail, looking towards a ghostly judge.

Marcello, as on that night on the *Leonardo da Vinci*, I had had quite a bit to drink. I wasn't sure whether he was real or not.

'How do you plead?' the ghost said. 'Guilty or not guilty?'

I was terrified, until I realised the ghost was a man.

'Guilty!' I said. 'Of anything and everything.'

How did it feel to be guilty of child-murder, prostitution, false-pretences? Or shop-lifting? Now *there* was a presentiment! Or even murder.

'You're Henry Walton, aren't you?'

'And you're Elizabeth Edwardes. The parson's daughter.' He sounded more than a little drunk. 'You're with anyone?'

'No, not really.'

He left the judge's seat and came towards me.

'I really should be in the dock,' he said. 'I wouldn't like to judge anyone. With the criminal, I have a certain sympathy.'

That remark (presentiment again!) seemed to create a sudden intimacy.

110

Music throbbed faintly from above.

'You'd like to dance? I'm not much good at it myself.'

'I'm not a dancer, either.'

'You'd like a drink?'

'I think I've had enough.'

'Then how about going for a drive?'

'You're sure you want to?' What I really meant was, was he able to, drive, I mean.

But he seemed to sober up on the way. Anyhow, it was only a short drive.

To that walled house of his, on the edge of the town. He had his own quarters over the stables, and the house was very quiet, but I had a strange feeling that we were being watched. (Afterwards, when I knew the set-up better, I was sure it must have been by Hannah, the maid.)

He led me to his room, filled with gadgets and golf-clubs. I don't think I actually wanted sex, from him or anyone. I was really frightened of it. But he seemed gentle at first and, as he closed the door and poured whisky, I thought, I don't care what he does. I don't care!

I let him undress me, which he did as if he were raping me. My clothes were torn. I didn't care. I was even becoming excited.

But when he started to make love to me – nothing! Just warm sticky liquid on my thighs. And he was crying!

He drove me home around 3 a.m., just about the time the Town Hall dance would be over, so Daddy wasn't at all surprised. His light was still on.

'Did you have a good time?' he said.

'Lovely.'

Two or three days later, just before I was about to return south, the phone rang.

'Miss Edwardes? This is Mrs Walton, *Henry's* mother! I would be delighted if you'd have tea with me. Are you, by any chance, free this afternoon?'

And so Henry became engaged to the prim and proper parson's daughter, and he gave me a photograph of himself, to take away, in a silver frame.

That, Marcello, happened more than eight years ago.

Eleven

Amore,

This is the England I imagined? Beefeaters, thatched cottages, the King's Road, the Queen? This up-North England, drab and grey, is light-years from any travel poster. But to me it's exciting. Because I'm on a mission?

On the way, she was always showing me Roman remains, archaeological bits and pieces, which in spite of being very inanimate, reminded me of you, you gorgeous Roman, you! You've never been to England, have you? So I'm your eyes and ears, and, I suppose, a bit of your imagination, too. Ah, togetherness! Except that you sent me away.

Marcello, as you predicted, she is falling in love with me. She resists, but it's hopeless. She shows exaggerated concern for my health, what I eat and drink, whether I feel hot or cold. She worries about my bowels, whether my period is late (it wasn't, you'll be relieved to know). She tucks me up in bed at night and made sure, on the way up here, that I didn't miss early morning tea. (A strange English ritual to which she attaches a good deal of importance.)

Marcello, she spoils me as you never did. She even cares about my 'education', going out of the way to show me old castles, churches, country houses. The trip has been like a history lesson, and sometimes I have been bored. But she cares! I'll say that for her. Do you?

We slept and ate in some cute old inns. You're jealous? No? You should be. It was like taking a trip with a lover who was 'saving himself' for the wedding night. With difficulty! Every morning and evening, she'd find some excuse to come in while I was taking a shower. First she was soaping my back, and yesterday, my breasts! It wasn't

113

unpleasant. Do you suppose I could become gay for good? You did tell me to be absolutely honest and frank about everything. Well, I am growing quite fond of her (she *needs* me so!) and sometimes I feel absolutely terrible about what we're doing to her. It's as if we were making her into some kind of sacrifice. You know, cherished before the end! And all the time I feel you're watching me, like a high priest supervising one of his minions. It's that look you have. Hypnotic. If you started a sect in California, baby, you'd have them paying ten dollars just to touch your clothes! As usual, I'm losing myself, thinking of you. (But was I really the youngest?)

Amore, this place where *he* lives! The town, I mean. The small houses, streets and streets of them, tiny, usually with outside loos, marching up and down the hillsides; and the mills among them that once spun cotton, cotton from *America*! (and Egypt, too, I suppose), like ugly palaces of long-dead kings. And, beyond the town, the moors, bleak and barren and mysterious, like something out of the Brontes, and, of course, they didn't live far from here, did they? It's all so dramatic and strange, I feel I'm sleep-walking, remembering a movie I once saw, but can't remember the name.

His house! Well, it's on the edge of town, surrounded by a wall about ten feet high. Inside now, I feel somehow I've gotten into the enemy camp. Part one of mission completed!

And his mother. I don't believe she even knows we're here. She's sick, occupies her own wing of the house. Cancer. A terminal case. Nurses, day and night.

And of course Henry, himself! How can I begin? With a physical description? Well, he's about five foot ten and, as far as one can tell, under the tweed suit he hasn't a bad body. And he does look quite a bit like James, my old boy-friend, remember? He has a small paunch and when he remembers it, he pulls in his stomach muscles so that he

114

looks like a caricature of a prize fighter entering the ring. His vaguely brown hair is thinning. His mouth is fleshy, but because he's so psychologically mixed up, he keeps pursing his lips and then thrusts them out again when he realises what he is doing. The effect is comic, and pathetic, too. His ears are small. He doesn't know what to do with his hands. He sweats. He drinks a lot. Whisky.

All this paints an unpleasant portrait? Wrong. He's not unattractive. If only he could get away from this place. But he never will, of course. He has wit and intelligence, but some sort of mental blockage. He lives in this house of ghosts, a willing prisoner, haunted day and night. He will join them. The ghosts, I mean.

When we arrived in Miss E's tiny car, he seemed terrified and delighted, anxious to get us inside, safe behind that high brick wall. Because someone might see us? Or because we might escape?

My room is on the first floor, crammed with Victorian bric-a-brac, stuffed birds in cages, bed-sheets trimmed with crochet and embroidered with the family initials. It has a shuttered, unlived in feel. Am I the first person to occupy it for generations? I have the creepy feeling that someone must have died in this enormous mahogany bed in which I am writing this letter. It is not a bed for birth, or love. Only death. The light is very dim, which is just as well. If Miss E saw a light under the door she would probably come in, and of course I don't want her to know I am sending reports to you.

Amore, after we had been shown our rooms by an old crone of a family retainer (who disapproves of me, I'm sure, and Miss E, too!), and we'd freshened up and then really met him, boy, was it weird! It was like being entertained by a conjurer. His part of the house is a sort of gadget museum. Musical cigarette boxes; bottles that play tunes when you pour from them; pencils that are really flashlights, and vice versa; lighters that fire like guns. He has

115

rigged up the lighting of his living-room so that it changes with the changes in the mood-music, like in a disco. He must have spent a fortune. It's like being in the place of imprisonment of a very rich and very privileged nut, guilty of some very odd form of insanity.

We came down for dinner, Miss E and I, at the same time, she wearing one of her new Roman outfits. At first, Henry was almost speechless, looking at her and me as if we'd arrived from another planet. (I was wearing a see-through number.) He poured enormous drinks and, instead of talking, demonstrated his gadgets. He seems to turn everything into a gadget. His cigarettes. He has them hand-made by some small, *very* exclusive firm in Jermyn Street, London. He offers them from a gold case which he keeps in a sort of chamois sachet. Ditto, his gold lighter. And his gold cigarette-holder! *Amore,* do you suppose he keeps his penis in a little sachet, too? When that thought struck me, I got the giggles. Both he and Miss E thought it was the effect of whisky on a minor.

Something important, possibly, to the matter in hand. What happened – or didn't happen – when he and Miss E greeted each other. I had forgotten to mention. They didn't kiss! Not even a cheek-peck. And they're supposed to be engaged! To him, she's obviously some new, different kind of person. (Though not necessarily more desirable – his eyes are on me, or rather what you call my good Italian breast-work!) But he's puzzled, intrigued by the change.

'Rome?' he stuttered when finally he became articulate. 'Italy?'

'Yes.'

'Really?' Miss E might have been to the moon.

'You've never been to Italy, Henry?' I said.

'N-never!' He might have been disclaiming knowledge of the devil. He half looked at Miss E. 'You've given up teaching?'

'Yes.'

116

'B-but ... ?'

'Why?'

'Well, yes.'

'Well, as your mother is dying, there's no reason why we shouldn't get married. Finally!' She made a gesture that took in the whole house. She was a little drunk, but doing nicely, exactly as rehearsed. 'You'll want to go on living here?'

'What?'

'I mean, after we're married?'

'I hope you'll invite me to the wedding,' I said, stirring things up. 'I don't know if I'd be able to make it, but it would be nice to be asked.'

Near-panic, dispelled only by a display of gadgets that included a clockwork cockerel which crowed the French national anthem. Of course she doesn't really want to marry him, she wants me. And he doesn't want to marry her. But he feels committed, mostly to Mama. Fortunately, however, Mama's chosen, prissy, sexless schoolteacher has unaccountably become a tramp. He is very confused, and I don't blame him. All this, and my presence, too! Tragic and comic, isn't it?

Amore, as of this moment, I can't imagine what I'm going to do to provoke the situation you need. But I'm sure I'll be the catalyst. Perhaps I'll even change my nature and become *involved.* With her? With him? Would you mind? Or merely get a kick out of the idea?

This first evening dissolved in an alcoholic fog, nothing decided, everything possible, the whole situation, as you imagined, absolutely *seething*! If only we could talk. And, of course, do other things. Like screw, for example! But I'm all alone in a foreign land, and I guess it's entirely up to me. An experiment in human relations, as you said. Sort of research. And I'm happy to be of assistance to you, sir, senor, signore, *amore*! I am also, you'll be relieved to hear, still feeling ruthless and cruel enough, I mean to do what-

117

ever has to be done.

You miss me a little? I dote. Just thinking about you makes me throb, you know where. I can't wait to get back, mission completed, and get my reward ... Oh yes, and I have plans, for us. In the States. How does that sound? ... It's after one and about twenty minutes since I took a pill (no, I won't forget the other one tomorrow morning after brushing my teeth). Tomorrow morning I'll also try and get this, after a nourishing English breakfast, to the post...

Twelve

Marcello,

We have arrived! And I am writing to you secretly, as promised, though I have had to wait till after 1.30 a.m. to do it. Our little American's light (she is in the next room) has only now just gone off. (Barefooted, I was watching the slit under the door!)

Suddenly, I am horribly afraid. Because his mother is dying under this very roof? She could go at any time, apparently. I have never seen anyone dead; both my parents died in hospital and I could not bring myself to look at them. The guilt of not wanting to see them still haunts me.

Henry seems indifferent to the idea of her death; both elated and frightened by the prospect of freedom. This place terrifies me. Must I marry this man? Why didn't you love me while I was in Rome? Or, if you couldn't, why didn't you find me a lover? Perhaps you did. You found me Dusty. Is that the reason men find me unattractive? They just *know*! I have touched her body, and my limbs turn to jelly. Is that what I really am? I have cut my hair short. Dusty said it suits me and kissed me, on the lips, to celebrate the change. But does she love?

Marcello, I could not write like this if I were not a little drunk. This first evening, we all went to bed a little drunk, and me, very jealous. Henry could not keep his eyes off our little American. And she responded, running her fingers coquettishly through her hair, stretching her body like a contented cat, brushing herself against him, touching his hand over the dinner-table.

I tried to talk to Henry about our future, mostly, I

confess, to draw his attention away from her. But actually the idea of living here with Henry appals me.

After the death (Hannah, the old housekeeper permitting, if she does not retire, suitably pensioned, to her Welsh valley), am I to be queen of this mausoleum? ... It is very late. I must try to sleep. I will write more tomorrow ...

Thursday/Friday night. Anyway, 1.50 a.m. This morning, saying, untruly, that I wanted to visit an aged relative, I went for a walk through this town I knew so well as a child and young girl. In reality, I was unable to bear looking at them together.

At breakfast, he tried to be polite to me. But all his attention was really centred on her. And she encourages him. He is ridiculous and pathetic at the same time, treating me not as a fiancee, but as a sister who, returning from foreign parts, has thoughtfully brought him a new gadget which happens to be female.

Soon after breakfast, they went off together in his car. And I took my walk.

It surprises you, Marcello, that it can be hot in this northern part of the world, so close to the farthest limits of the Roman Empire? Would you suffer, so far from home, as perhaps the legionaries suffered, missing the sights, sounds, smells of the Mediterranean? (When next you need to experience 'hell', why not come here rather than New York? Or perhaps you are already getting the essential experience, regarding our little American and me as your reporters and ambassadors?)

Anyway, I took my walk; away from this house on the edge of the moor, into the centre of town, with its public library, its public baths with separate entrances for 'Males' and 'Females', past the chain stores and super-markets, and, of course, the Town Hall in whose court room I had that first encounter with Henry. Remember?

In the town centre there is a pub called The Magnet, much tarted up by the brewery recently. Henry said something about it last night.

I saw his car parked outside.

The bar is divided into two halves. Eenie-Meenie! I eased open the left-hand door, couldn't see them, and went in.

I ordered a gin and tonic, *sotto voce*, because I could see (through a convenient mirror) and hear them on the other side. She was drinking Coke, and he whisky, flamboyant and already a little drunk, luxuriating in her exotic presence. See what I've got! A real live American girl, wearing red pants, and with long golden, sort of dusty-gold, hair!

Henry, apparently, is an habitue of The Magnet, treated with both deference and subtle intimacy.

The big-bosomed barmaid with the lacquered hair says to Dusty, 'You're from the States, dear? Now that's where I'd like to go. You're touring in these parts? Can't imagine why. Give me the bright lights, a bit of life!'

'That,' says the landlord, 'is something you could easily get just where you don't want it!'

And everyone in the bar laughs. Except me. I feel sick. She can't possibly find him attractive? It's impossible. She must simply be demonstrating his foolishness for my benefit. But that *can't* be so. She doesn't know I'm here.

I had another quick gin-and-tonic and then fled from the place, afraid of being seen, detected. I fled to the bed-side of my aged aunt, but it was all sickness and bed-pans; and after that I fled into a movie and relaxed a little in Mexico, a Western in which death came as naturally and red as the sunrise and men escaped either into domesticity or by riding off, alone but free, into the sunset, and the sound-track pumped out a message, about love and life and death, I couldn't define.

I was home first. Early this evening, before dinner, she came to my room, very animated, I thought, but also nervous, as if what she was saying somehow *mattered*.

'He's asked me to play golf with him tomorrow morning.'

'Well, why not?'

'You don't mind?'

'Of course not. Why should I? You have clubs?'

'He has a half-set he used as a boy.'

'Oh, good.'

We were looking at one another in the dressing-table mirror, her image ghostly behind me. She placed a hand on my shoulder, and I covered hers with mine.

'It's all right?'

'Of course.'

'But he's your fiance. He's neglecting you.'

I said, 'I don't really care about Henry. It's you I worry about.'

I got up, turned to face her. Fresh from the bath, she was wearing nothing but her dressing-gown, and suddenly she was in my arms. I was pressing my mouth to hers and she let me kiss her. Feverishly, I loosened her dressing-gown and her nipples became erect and ripe in my mouth . . . Marcello, does this make you angry, or merely amused? Perhaps, with your jaded appetites, it merely excites you? But when I tried gently to push her towards the bed, she as gently resisted.

'No . . . not yet . . .'

'No?' I was devastated.

'Let's have a little fun first. With Henry.' She laughed, suddenly all young schoolgirlish and kittenish. 'Anyway, in this house, I simply couldn't. Too spookish, too deathly! You know?'

I did indeed. The mere mention of death switched me off. I froze.

But she used my comb, my perfume, my lipstick, giving brief, substitute satisfaction.

'So the golf date is all right? You're sure you don't mind?'

'No. But what do you want from him?'

'You don't know?'

122

'Well, you seem to find him attractive, as a man.'

Our little American dissolved into helpless laughter.

'It's so amusing?'

'Not really. What I'm after is your liberation.'

She was now using my lipstick with intense concentration.

'Liberation?'

'Come and watch.'

'Watch? You mean on the golf-course, tomorrow?'

'From a discreet distance.'

Dusty now had her face cosmetically adjusted to her satisfaction, the outlines of her mouth drawn rather more sharply than usual, so that her appearance was changed, my dear Marcello, in a sinister way I cannot describe. Perhaps you, the writer, can find the words. But again I was afraid. Suddenly she was a different person, an actress ready to face camera or footlights, aloof; a creature of a strange world, compounded by both reality and fantasy. And nightmare.

'And then?' I said.

'We should leave this place.' She stroked me cheek. 'There will be nothing more for us here.'

Hypnotised, I said, 'No, I don't want to stay.'

'Good. Then we leave tomorrow. You'd better pack. Do it tonight. I'll have my bag ready, too.'

'All right.'

'Put all our things into your car. Then we can leave right after the game. Won't it be good to be on the road together again?'

I shivered. All I could think of, Marcello, was her and me together, in the snug, chintzy bedroom of some country inn. I have just finished packing and will post this, I hope, tomorrow morning, before leaving for the golf-course. His mother, apparently, has taken a turn for the worse. I cannot stay in a house of death ... Marcello, why am I so *afraid*?

Thirteen

Earlier, this evening, *amore*, after we had all supposedly gone to bed, I tiptoed to the door of his private sanctum, wearing only my dressing-gown, not even a nightdress, my feet bare.

Though my plans are laid for tomorrow, I wanted to raise the emotional temperature a little more, though it's pretty high already!

This evening at dinner, he played footsie with me under the table, and Miss E was doing ditto with me. Piquant, no?

When I said, quite casually, that we would be leaving soon, perhaps even tomorrow, he became very *distrait* and said he wouldn't hear of it. When Miss E went to watch the news on TV, he tried to kiss me ... I was discouraging, but friendly.

But back to the corridor outside his room. My hand was actually touching the knob, all set for a silent, dramatic entrance, when I heard his voice.

' "A nincompoop!" that's what she called me. "A good-for-nothing! What will happen at the mill when you're at the head of the boardroom table, I just don't know!" And she sat there, in her rocking-chair, as she always sat, crochet-needles flashing and clicking and jabbing, producing their endless cotton ectoplasm that now drips from the sheets of every bedroom in the house, including the bed on which she now lies dying . . .'

The voice came and went, *amore*, now louder, now softer. And then, suddenly, I understood.

He was playing back a tape, his recorded autobiography.

Suppose there was more, much more, of it? Suppose I

could get my hands on it. The very thing you need!

I heard the clink of glass on glass as he poured himself another drink, and then footsteps, so close that I was certain he was about to throw open the door. I almost died!

Suddenly, I didn't want to see him that night ... The voice continued after a moment, but I didn't listen. I fled back to my room and lay on top of my bed, breathless, thinking.

Suppose I could steal those tapes! Tomorrow. Before or after?

Just imagine what they could do for your (our?) book?

Fourteen

Excellent material from both my correspondents! I'm especially pleased with Miss E. In spite of her delicious state of terror, she keeps her wits about her. Lucid, detailed, exact, she obviously tries hard to be objective about herself and her motives. I have of course edited her material a little, cleaning up her somewhat hasty style, filled in some background and characterisation, added some dialogue to improve readability – but I have avoided, I hope, any 'literary' flourishes.

I have been working on the material with unaccustomed concentration, shut up for hours at a time in my study, ever since it started to come through, including, of course, the earlier parts of Miss E's story. Some of what 'I' have written I have shown to Clara. She is enthusiastic, discusses the characters with me and, I have to admit, I find her analyses of them – that is, from the stand-point of a professional psychiatrist – quite invaluable and revealing. At one time I did consider incorporating her observations as footnotes, but rejected the idea as such academic embellishments, I thought, would discourage the average reader, and it is sales, of course, as well as a *succes d'estime* in a new genre, that I am after.

A few days ago, I was feeling so excited by the book that I was on the point of sending a carbon copy of the script, even though incomplete, to Milan, hoping Caesare would reciprocate my and Clara's enthusiasm. But discretion prevailed. I have always disliked showing work in progress to anyone, or even talking about it. This was, indeed, the first time I have even shown an incomplete work to my wife. But I know I can rely on her discretion. These notes of mine will, of course, be deleted in the final version (they are inserted in the script now, merely to clarify my ideas); my own contribution to the plot will be minimised. This, I am convinced, is not cowardice, merely modesty. What is happening could have happened anyway, or so I tell myself. Or is this hypocritical?

But what *is* happening? I have an indescribable feeling of expectancy. I cannot, at the moment, imagine the story's end. But it will, I hope, as in all good mysteries, be seen, when it comes, as both inevitable and a surprise. The characters have taken charge, which is entirely as it should be. Now I am merely the reporter.

I await the arrival of the post as if my very existence depended on it, as, in a way, it does. The deed – what deed? – is done? How will Miss E and our little American react to their complicity in crime – as crime, as a non-Christian, I pray there must be. For drama's sake, amen! Neither of them must go to the police with an attack of conscience, which would be banal and ruin the story. I would hate to have to invent a 'better' ending.

Today, I am particularly on edge. The post has just arrived. Nothing from England. The last letter was from the little one, written before the act, whatever the act is. Her news about Henry's tapes was very exciting, and I will, of course, incorporate them in the script in what I consider the best places to intensify the drama. (Unfortunately, I do not possess a recorder of the type Dusty describes, and last night I asked Clara to advance me the money to buy one.)

But another postal strike threatened. Though, generally, I am in sympathy, as an intellectual, with the workers, there are times when their demands, however legitimate, are damned inconvenient, and I sometimes think that perhaps we in Italy (I don't say Italians, because I am not convinced we are one people), once again need a strong man. The strong criminal who commits the necessary acts of violence and intolerance for all.

I hear the door, opening softly. It cannot be my daughter, who always bursts in, especially since her return from the Dolomiti, with noisy, youthful energy, looking prettier than ever, suddenly. I think she must have a lover, which makes me feel old, yet more resigned to the vicarious delights of writing about the sexual adventures of others. I feel a chapter of my life closing ... No, it will be Clara, returning punctually, from the clinic. She will hear my typewriter, and not wishing to disturb me, go straight to the kitchen. Clara! Only a few weeks ago, it would have been inconceivable. I actually look forward to your evening-shadowed, secret return.

Fifteen

Marcello,

My hand shakes so, I can hardly write. But our little Dusty says I must write. To you! (She has taken a sleeping pill and is out of it.) But you are the only one in whom I could possibly confide, and she knows it. Marcello, what should I do? All my instincts tell me to go to the police. But what about her? What would they *do* to her? Perhaps I would never see her again. And that is unthinkable, impossible, inconceivable!

Marcello, this morning I said good-bye to Henry. He kissed me chastely on both cheeks and agreed it was better if we did nothing definite about getting married for the time being, his mother being so ill. He seemed contrite that he had neglected me during my visit and mumbled vague apologies. I said, not to worry.

I just wanted to be away, alone again with our little one. To get out of that house, away from death, and breathe fresh air! Only that mattered.

But Henry said I should say good-bye also to his mother. I hadn't even said hello. I suppose Hannah must have told her I was in the house. Well, I couldn't refuse, could I? I mean I was supposed to be marrying her son, after she had gone, taking over the role of jailer!

Sick-rooms terrify me, Marcello. It was awful. The darkness, the claustrophobia of the approaching crypt, the smell! At 10 a.m., no daylight.

Under a very dim lamp, the nurse, a youngish woman of about my own age, was reading a paperback, a discreet, self-effacing traveller on a night-train. But when she saw me hesitating at the door (Henry was waiting outside), she got up and led me, hand in hand, towards the bed. She knew the courtesies.

I think she, Mama, recognised me almost at once. Though no doubt she was sedated, her eyes still had, miraculously, that gimlet quality that had so terrified me at our first meeting.

Petrified, I sat down on the chair close to the bed, and took her hand. I once touched, reluctantly, a snake. It was like that.

The nurse stood at the other side of the bed and placed a glass of water to her lips.

The lips moved.

'Bend closer,' the nurse said, and obediently I placed my ear close to her mouth. It was like approaching a mummy in an Italian church, of a centuries-dead saint. His mother a saint? Anyway, she was a manifestation of an almost supernatural will. I have never been so terrified. That is, not until later this morning! Marcello, Marcello, what shall I do? If only you were here to help me!

At first I could not make out the words. Terror closed my ears. But then, as I fought back panic, they began to register in my brain. '. . . not long . . . you must protect him . . . you are strong enough . . . ?'

Me? The little teacher? Though no doubt it was because I'm a teacher that she chose me as her successor, in the first place. A person prim and proper and asexual. How stupid can the wise ones be!

I mumbled something, perhaps a promise impossible to keep, and fled, after forcing myself to kiss that clammy forehead. Did she smile? Or was the drawing back of the lips only another expression of pain?

Marcello, I think one reason why Henry had not himself entered the death-chamber was that he was already dressed for golf. His sportive appearance would have seemed unseemly to his mother (would she have noticed?), and to the nurse (though she had resumed her reading even before I

130

left the room)?

Why am I writing first such comparatively unimportant details? Only, I suppose, because I am trying to get the exact sequence of events clear in my own mind, to help us both understand.

The arrangement was for Henry and our little American to drive to the golf-course in his Rover, while I, in my old faithful Morris, was to meet them, an hour or so later, at the club-house.

After the encounter with Mama, I returned, shaking, to my room to make sure I had forgotten nothing. (We were to leave immediately after their game.)

Passing the open door of our little one's room, I saw her having difficulty, apparently, in closing her suitcase. I went to help her, but she pushed me away, almost roughly.

'What have you got in there?'

'Nothing important. Can't you ever leave me alone, even for a moment!'

I was hurt, but seconds later, the suitcase safely closed, she was brushing her lips against my cheek. 'I'm sorry, darling. Truly. You forgive?'

'Of course.'

'Don't forget.'

'Forget?'

'To look out for us on the course. Henry says there's a shelter near the ninth tee you know about. Yes?'

'Yes.'

'Give us about an hour and a half.'

She left and, ten minutes later, I myself left the house, with an enormous sense of relief. I was escaping. But to what? The terror persisted.

That countryside is quite unlike anything I think you know in Italy, Marcello. The moors, bleak and barren and grey, pile up behind the town like a huge immobile sea, treeless, tinted with purple only at the purple time of the year. But there are patches of green, like green beaches on the edge of this sea. On one of these beaches, lies the golf-course.

I was to give them ninety minutes to reach the ninth tee. So, instead of driving straight to the course, which is about three miles out of town, I drove to one of those moorland villages which consists of nothing more than a cluster of houses, a tiny church and graveyard, and a pub.

I did consider entering the church, to get out of the still-oppressive heat. But the pub, with its thick stone walls and whitewashed bar, would be equally cool and offer more immediate refreshment.

There was a small white Alfa (ah, Italy, again!) parked outside, and just two women inside, drinking gin. One small and fluffy and feminine; the other tweedy and protective.

I knew they were watching, listening, as I also asked for gin. Does it show? Did *you* know, Marcello, from the first moment you saw me?

They seemed suddenly to draw closer together, as if drawn by mutually protective jealousy. Did even the land-lord know? Is that why he seemed unfriendly, serving me as if I were yet another unwelcome intruder in that un-changing village where males and females, married, properly paired, ate and slept together in their cottages and finally lay together in the indissoluble wedlock of the churchyard?

I tried to concentrate on the newspaper I had bought, but my brain registered nothing but their female presence, and the fact that the small blonde somehow reminded me of Dusty. Just above my head, tormented insects struggled hopelessly on the fly-paper.

At breakfast, I had eaten almost nothing and the gin went immediately to my head. But I still had time to kill

132

and ordered another. While paying, I noticed that I had only a few pounds left (my trip to Rome had been expensive), and I knew my funds at the bank were dangerously low. Our little one has told me not to worry about money. There is plenty more, she says, where hers comes from. But this makes me feel terrible. I feel protective about her.

Protective! Why wasn't I protecting her now. The fear fought and won against the comforting glow of the gin, and I fled from the bar. Sixty-five minutes gone!

There is a narrow dirt road that runs along part of the boundary of the golf-course, and from one particular place on that road it is possible to see over practically the whole course.

I stopped the little Morris and stared over the whole expanse.

No one!

Had they lied to me? Perhaps they had planned not to come to the course at all. Perhaps at that moment, they were together in a bedroom at some local hotel. Perhaps they were in the club-house, having decided not to play because of the heat.

Marcello, close to the ninth tee there is this sort of shelter, clearly visible from where I was standing. In fact, it is really an old farm building, a sort of barn, all that remains of an impoverished smallholding that was bought up to build the course.

The building has a sinister local reputation. Long ago, it had been the scene of some unspeakable crime. As a child, I was always terrified of the place; and even my father, God-fearing and woman-hating, playing a solitary round in mid-week, thinking of his sermon for Sunday, would avoid it unless the rain was particularly heavy. (He made me accompany him 'for the exercise', but always hating me, I felt, throughout the long silences, because I was a girl and not a boy. And also because I reminded him of his wife, my mother, who ran away from him? Did I ever tell you that,

133

Marcello?) He would stand in the doorway, still imperfectly protected from the rain, and tell me not to go inside.

What nameless terrors did the place contain?

Why had Dusty mentioned the place that morning? Had she been *willing* me to go there?

Without making any conscious decision, I found myself walking towards it.

The door was slightly ajar. Timidly, I pushed it open wider, listening, and, hearing nothing, went inside. Out of the sun, I was suddenly cold, but it was a cold not entirely a matter of temperature. Out of childhood, chilling terrors came flooding back. I saw old newspapers, empty cans, the remains of a long-dead fire. Evidently the place was sometimes used by tramps. A rickety wooden staircase led to the upper floor.

For several seconds, I stood quite still, still listening. For what? Was that small, vague sound from up there only my imagination, or a trick of the wind?

I moved to the foot of the staircase. It was absurd to risk a leg, but I knew that I had to go up.

As my head came level with the upper floor, I stopped. This sound, half gasp, half cry, was not in my imagination. The only light came from small gaps in the rotten roof. My eyes still dazzled by the sunlight, I sensed rather than saw her, crouching in a corner.

'Dusty!'

She began to materialise, just a white face, it seemed, uttering small, pathetic animal noises.

I did not move from the staircase; my head was still at floor-level. She came towards me then, in a strange creeping manner, on hands and knees, and when her face was only inches from mine, she whispered, 'Henry's dead!'

I stared at her, stupidly.

'Dead,' she said again. 'He tried to make love to me and I laughed at him. He tried to stop me laughing and put his

134

hand over my mouth. So I hit him and went on hitting.'

I saw that her dress was torn, her hair a mess. She looked very young and suddenly I was reminded of the girl I taught once who, on a school excursion, had left the party and become involved in a motor accident, and I was both sorry for her, and angry, too, because she was guilty of a breach of discipline.

Suddenly I felt quite calm, able to cope. 'You're quite sure he's dead?' My concern at that moment was not for Henry. I was questioning an erring but likeable pupil.

'Yes, yes. I think so. I *know* so. He's just lying there.'

I looked towards the corner from which she had crept. I fancied I could make out the greenish colour of the shirt Henry had been wearing that morning, even the shape of a trousered leg.

'Don't look!' Dusty said. 'It's horrible.'

I could not have brought myself to look, anyway. That morning I had already looked upon death. But my brain became increasingly clear. Terror was now defined.

'Did anyone see you come in here?'

'I don't think so.'

I stared at her hands. She was still wearing golfing gloves. 'You kept those on? All the time, even in here?'

'Yes, yes.'

'What did you hit him with?'

'The putter. I hit him. Again and again.'

'Where is it?'

She glanced back. 'Over near the body.'

'Get it!'

'But I don't want...'

'I said, get it!'

Obediently, on hands and knees as she had come to me, she went and retrieved the club, holding it gingerly by the leather grip. There was a red stain on the head.

'Where's the rest of your set?'

'In his car. We decided not to play, because of the heat. I

135

brought the putter just to get a little practice on the greens.'

'There's nothing else of yours there?'

'No.'

'Purse, lipstick, handkerchief, anything like that?'

'No, no. I'm sure.'

'Did you leave anything of yours in his car.'

'No. My suitcase is in your car.'

This was true. I suddenly felt foolish for not opening hers, while I was alone, to discover why it had been so difficult to close.

'All right. Come down now.'

'Where are we going?'

'Never mind.' I was quite sharp with her, the school-mistressy disciplinarian. 'Come!'

Meekly, she followed me down that rotten staircase. From the doorway I peered out, but saw nothing, no one.

Five minutes later, we were sitting in my car.

'So he's dead.' She half smiled. 'You're pleased?'

'Pleased?'

'To be rid of him. Am I not good to you?' She leaned over and kissed my cheek – nearly all her old bounce was back, suddenly and miraculously. 'And you're good to me.'

Marcello, she was right. Henry was no longer a problem, and for that I had only Dusty to thank.

'Of course you were egging him on,' I said. 'But I never thought him capable of it.'

'Capable of what?'

'Rape. That is what he attempted, isn't it?'

I twisted the starter.

In five minutes we were back on the highway, the road leading right away from the town, that house, Henry's dying mother and the life I might have had if Henry had been alive.

For a long time we did not speak, but I kept trying to imagine the scene of the crime. The physical details. Whose

136

in fact *was* the crime? His? Dusty's? Or mine?

As you must have realised, Marcello, I have this obsession with crime, with sin, with the processes of law, imagining myself, most often, as the prisoner in the dock. Always I have been certain that, one day, imagination would become reality. (The shop-lifting episode was a mere foretaste of the real thing.) Since that first meeting with Henry, in a court-room, you remember, I have attended many sessions in many courts, an avid member of the public in whose name justice is done. I have followed cases of petty theft, grievous bodily harm, indecent exposure. I have listened to some of the more unsavoury divorce cases. To a rape case at the Assizes. The ladies in the public gallery were asked by the considerate judge if they wished to leave the court before the essential evidence was heard. Not a woman moved. Including me. I was astonished, enthralled, nauseated. The physical detail necessary to prove whether the girl involved had fought for her honour, or merely passively accepted a half-wished-for assault. The descriptions of scratches, bruises, lacerations, given by the police surgeon! The torn and blood-stained under-clothing produced in evidence! Exhibit A: panties. Exhibit B: stockings. Exhibit C: see-through bra, etc., ... And the girl herself, reduced to tears by the severity of the cross-examination, and offered a sip of water, when perhaps brandy would have been more welcome, by the same kindly, but implacable judge!

A hundred miles later, without asking if she was hungry, I turned into one of those automated eating-places on the motorway south.

Dusty ate a hamburger and drank a glass of milk with surprising appetite.

As she finished, I said, 'You haven't answered my question.'

'Question?' She put more ketchup on the last morsel of hamburger.

137

'I mean, whether he tried to rape you?'

'Of course he did. I told you.'

'Henry never seemed to be a violent man. Quite the contrary.'

'About men you never can tell. One reason we came on this trip was to discover what kind of man Henry really is. I mean, was.' Dusty looked at my untouched food. 'Why don't you eat?'

'I'm not hungry.'

'Because you're worried?' She placed her hand over mine, and I confess I melted with love and concern. 'About me? Don't be. We can still go to the police, if you like. It's not too late. We can just say we panicked and ran. A perfectly natural reaction. D'you suppose I could have another hamburger?'

I gave the order.

'What do you suppose they could do to me?'

'That depends on whether they believe your story.'

'You think it's unbelievable?'

'You laughed at him and he tried to stop you laughing. How?'

'He tried to put his hands over my mouth, and when I struggled he put them round my throat.'

'So you were very close, physically, I mean?'

'Obviously.'

'And you were holding the putter all the time?'

Dusty seemed to lose interest in the second hamburger. She stared at me reproachfully. 'You think I *murdered* him?'

'To swing a club with enough force to kill him, you'd have to be at least a yard away. So you can't have been all *that* close.'

'In the struggle, I must have pushed him away.'

'So hitting him wasn't really necessary, was it? So why?'

'Because suddenly he disgusted me.'

'But why did you hit him so many times. Wouldn't one blow have been enough?'

Dusty pushed her plate away. 'Why are you torturing me?'

'Dearest darling,' I said, 'this is nothing compared with what the police would do to you. Why so many times?'

'I don't know. I just went on hitting.'

'He didn't try to defend himself?'

'Not really. He seemed to be enjoying it.'

'That's ridiculous.'

'Is it? Then what are you saying. That I went sort of crazy? Is that what the police would say?'

'I don't know what the police would say. But it's a line of defence your counsel might have to consider. You would be examined, by doctors, psychiatrists. Darling, darling!' I squeezed her hand. 'They should examine me, too. Why did I let you go with him? Why?'

'Because we were conducting a sort of experiment. Remember?'

So I was equally guilty. Being older and presumably wiser, more so!

We were becoming interesting, in our emotional involvement, to other consumers of hamburgers, fish and chips, cottage pie, custard tart and trifle, and weak very un-Italian coffee, Marcello.

'Come,' I said. And we returned to the car.

On the runway of the motorway again, from which there is no take-off, no sudden airborne freedom, she said, 'No one saw us going in here. Anyone could have killed him.'

'Some hippy?'

'Why not?'

'But why murder?'

'Isn't that the kind of crime that's "in" these days? No motive. But if there has to be one, just "protest"!'

'Not in England.'

'I thought you might say that.'

Something glittered suddenly, on her lap. Henry's lighter, as it was drawn from its chamois jacket. Then his cigarette holder and the 24-carat case. 'I have his money, too,' Dusty said. 'About £23 and some small change. So the motive could also be theft.'

'You emptied his pockets before I arrived on the scene?' I was aghast.

'To save time.' Dusty lit a cigarette. 'There was a crack in the wall. I saw you coming. Anyway, we *had* planned the rendezvous, remember?'

My complicity was established, beyond doubt. Her hand touched mine as it rested on the lever as I changed gear.

'You're rid of him,' she said. 'Finally! Isn't that what you wanted?'

Marcello, it *is* what I wanted, isn't it? I'm free? Our little one has done what was necessary. For me. So I am responsible.

My love for her suddenly made me feel weak, almost ill with adoration.

I had determined to lose ourselves that evening in the anonymity of London, but I was quite unable to drive any further. I turned off the motorway at the next exit and found this hotel, all Tudor and brass and reconstituted Olde-England, that caused our rather sleepy, little American to cry out with pleasure, like any other trans-Atlantic tourist. The events of the morning receded into nightmare.

She kissed me good night, chastely but affectionately, and took her Mogadon. At that moment, I felt nothing for her but tenderness. Then, as soon as she was asleep, I started to write to you. But first I looked into her suitcase. The only unusual things I saw were three or four cassettes. I can't imagine what is on them or how she obtained them.

I shall post this as soon as we reach London tomorrow. I am calmer now. But if I could not write to you, Marcello, I'd die!

140

Sixteen

Amore!

Forgive the small silence, but suddenly I am engulfed. Anyway, Miss E has been, secretly, she imagined, to the post, so you have been kept up to date with developments.

Yes, it is done! I sort of persuaded him to attack me, and I hit him with a golf club. It may take a little time before the body is discovered. But that will give us a chance to get away.

So you have your real, bloody, unusually documented, strange crime. You have just what you wanted. You are pleased with me? I have done well?

As things stand at the moment, some imaginary hobo is supposed to be the culprit. Motive: robbery. But if that theory fails to convince the police and the evidence, in spite of all precautions (the club was thrown into a river more than a hundred miles from the scene of the crime!), somehow leads to us, Miss E is determined to take all the blame, even confessing to the actual murder. Motive: jealousy.

Isn't that sweet? A twist, as a writer, you will surely appreciate. But she is crazily in love with me, determined to protect my 'innocence' at all costs. But this is probably something of the sort you had in mind all along, you Machiavelli, you.

Anyway, within forty-eight hours I expect to be out of the country.

Listen, Daddy has arrived. Yes, here.

As soon as we arrived back in London, I went to American Express and there, sure enough at Clients' Mail, there was a note from him. 'Staying at the Hilton. Come as soon as you can.'

At first I was annoyed, I mean at the thought of being disturbed in the middle of our little game. But then I saw positive advantages in Daddy's arrival. There's the financial one of course (funds are running low and Daddy, guilt-ridden, will be generous). Second, I do have a taste for luxury, the creature comforts. Most important, it may solve the problem of what to do about Miss E. You see, *amore*, now I'm beginning to feel responsible for her! I like her, I really do. I might finally even go to bed with her. I don't actually want to (I might develop a taste for it!). What I mean is, Daddy's a very smart lawyer, and he'll probably be able to think of something. I won't tell him about the crime, of course. Just that Miss E is a nice person, sort of 'family' we ought to do something for, who needs help.

This will be a very short note. I'm writing on my knee in Amexco while Miss E (nervous tension or something we had to eat on the road?) has gone to the loo to be sick. I feel surprisingly relaxed. Mission completed!

Amore, I hope to see you in a few days. Please, please don't have any sex. You're best when you're hungry...

P.S. I'm sending Henry's tapes express!

Seventeen

Marcello, I can't understand her, our little American. I am utterly confused. She seems without feeling about what she has done – almost without memory. She doesn't even seem interested in the newspapers. This morning, at the country inn where we spent the night, I was up at seven, going over them, inch by inch, looking for some mention of the crime. Nothing! I had expected it to be all over the front page. People *must* be looking for him. That old servant guessed, knew about the triangle situation. They will start looking for him on the golf-course. Where else? She knew they were going to play.

I have been feeling terribly ill. Nervous reaction, probably. And I have just had my period, which always causes me a good deal of upset. (I'm sorry to talk about such things if it disgusts you.) Several times, I have thought of going to the police. But that would involve her, as a witness I suppose, even if I took full responsibility. Also, I confess I am terrified of losing her, or being separated. To add to my misery, I cannot be sure how she feels about me. Sometimes, she is warm and loving; sometimes, she acts as if I did not exist. She is coquettish. Men look at her. Women, too. It is exciting to be in her company, but also frightening because I'm afraid of losing her to even the most casual stranger.

You are probably wondering what course of action I had devised after the murder. The answer is, none. I hoped, prayed, we would not be implicated. But if it comes to that, I fully intend to take full responsibility. After all, with my 'criminal' record, the police will, probably rightly, suspect mental instability connected with sexual problems. So, I

143

killed him in a fit of violent jealousy. I confess, confess, confess... The nightmare world of my teens and twenties becomes reality. I will be terrified of prison, but reconciled. Because of its inevitability?

But first I must live a little. Ways of escape seem to be opening up.

As soon as we arrived in London, Dusty learned that her father is here, staying at the Hilton on whose stationery, as you see, I'm writing this. He is accompanied by his new wife, and old mistress, whose name is Beryl. She is a formidable red-head in her early twenties, and I think Dusty's father is a little afraid of her, just as he is afraid of Dusty, I mean for having married Beryl.

They occupy a luxurious suite with a view over the park; the iced Scotch flows in a never-ending fountain. Waiters are always arriving with succulent tit-bits. They pay a great deal of attention to me – so much, it's embarrassing. Dusty has told them some story about my having made her European trip into a memorable experience. They apparently think they owe me something.

In this plushy atmosphere, Dusty is in her element. She doesn't seem to have a care in the world. Tonight, the three of them have gone to the Playboy Club, just around the corner. They begged me to go, too. I pleaded a headache.

As you will have gathered, I am their guest. My room inter-connects with Dusty's. The TV is flickering soundlessly, the Scotch is at hand, and I write to you, to fill in the time until she returns. There's honesty!

They are full of trans-Atlantic bounce and plans. They have reservations in the Paris Hilton, the Athens Hilton, the Istanbul Hilton, the Tel-Aviv Hilton, the Cavalieri Hilton (Rome, as if you didn't know!) and the Castellana Hilton, Madrid, from where they will fly back to the States.

Marcello, they want me to accompany them on this Grand Tour! They want me to go back with them to the

States! Dusty's father says, that if I like America, he can obtain for me lucrative employment with a certain educational foundation whose lawyer he happens to be. Though he doubts if I would be so employed for long as he has a friend, recently divorced, who is crazy about English women and to whom I would be introduced very soon after my arrival in New York. Dusty's father has many friends, he is a man of considerable influence. He is of Italian origin, Sicilian, I believe. I wonder if you would like him, Marcello? He is called Angelo, as he insisted I called him from the moment of our meeting. He does not look particularly south Italian. He is tall, his hair grey, his features are very ad-man masculine. His hands, carefully manicured, are very beautiful. He wears coloured shirts and suits that seem to follow every line of his slim body. Dusty says he is fifty. He's perfectly controlled, in gesture, voice and, I think, thought. He give the impression that there is no problem he could not solve, for a large fee. He could offer absolution, forgiveness and even obliteration, of any crime. Can it be that he is the father confessor of your New York hell, Marcello?

He is proud of Beryl, his new hand-maiden. He makes little jokes about her being 'all-American', by which he means she isn't of Italian origin. But she walks with the smooth, swinging movements of the Italian woman, crossing from living-room to bedroom, clad only in a kimono, showing a great deal of leg. Dusty watches them together with faint amusement, and now and again, a wink at me. Her father is obviously relieved, and grateful, that she is taking his marriage so calmly.

Before they left for the Playboy, the phone was always ringing. Calls from New York, Los Angeles, Miami, Angelo taking them in an almost inaudible monotone when he was speaking English; more expressive when talking Italian. He jokes with the Italian waiter, who clearly thinks him *simpatico*.

Now here I am alone in my air-conditioned hotel capsule. Anonymous, cosseted, airborne on a vast current of ever-present, lubricating, fructifying, not-spoken-of, always-signed-for dollars; I am in another world, living on a higher plane of existence, inhabited only by those on whom the great God Buck has smiled. I am beginning to feel I understand Dusty at last, from her side of the pond, the 'Atlantic River'. Anything that happens in Europe, to her, doesn't really count; it isn't real. Killing isn't murder. Europe is a holiday, the place where the folks came from, one, two, three generations ago. Europe is a dream, a package; or, if you are rich enough, an individual tour.

And, apparently, I can join them. With a background of shop-lifting, complicity in murder and unwilling virginity, a whole new future opens up before me. If the police here don't catch up with me first.

Do you think I could be happier in America, Marcello? You know it better than I do, I mean 'rich' America. (I saw only the mid-West in winter, under snow. A lost school-teacher.) Am I not too European, no, too English to make the change? Too old? Cursed with a literary-historical memory, I tell myself that innumerable Englishmen (and women) have started afresh where the West begins, after careers in crime or dissent. But *me*, the minister's mixed-up daughter? Yes, I'd go if I felt our little one really cared. But does she? The decision depends on her. Soon, I hope, she will return. It is after 2 a.m.... I can't write any more now... The door between our rooms is open. I can hear her coming... I must hide this letter.

... She came straight into my room, turned on the radio, poured herself a generous three-fingers of Scotch.

'I needed that. When Daddy's around, it's more politic to drink Coke.'

'You had a pleasant evening?'

'I danced several times with a super man from Boston.' Jealousy hit me like a blow to the stomach. 'He wanted to see me again. But I said no, sorry, we're leaving, London, that is.'

She began dancing to the radio and undressing at the same time.

'Dusty!' I said. 'Darling, I love you.'

She stopped dancing and, wearing now only her pants and bra, said, 'I'm normal. At least, I think I am.'

I said in a low, tight whisper, 'How can you be sure unless you try?'

For a long moment she just stood there, not speaking, just looking at me.

'Darling,' I said, 'please.'

Suddenly, she drained the rest of the whisky.

'All right,' she said. 'Let's try.'

She put down her glass, reached behind her back to unfasten her bra, let it fall to the carpet. She stepped out of her pants and left them also on the floor. Then, quite naked, she went over to the bed. She lay down and looked at me.

'Come,' she said.

I took off my dressing-gown, the only thing I wore, and lay beside her, my heart thumping wildly. I kissed her mouth, her ears, her breasts, her belly. I gently opened her legs and kissed her. She lay supine and let me do with her anything I wanted, her limbs moving obediently at my slightest touch. And then, when I looked at her face at what should have been the moment of greatest pleasure, I saw that her eyes were open, staring fixedly at the ceiling, her expression perfectly calm, detached, perhaps slightly amused.

The fire in my own body died as if I had suddenly been plunged into icy water. I drew away from her with a kind of horror, filled with shame.

Then she seemed to become aware of me. She stretched languorously like a cat, got up from the bed.

She smiled and kissed me once on the lips.

'That was lovely,' she said, lying. 'Gosh, I'm sleepy. Good night.'

She padded off on bare feet to her own room, closing the door.

I just stood there, for I don't know how long. Then I poured myself a large whisky and lay on the bed, still warm and scented from her body, and sipped slowly. When I awoke just after eight o'clock, I knew quite clearly what I had to do.

The lift-boy, seeing me carrying my own bag, was not happy. Neither was the cashier.

'But you're Mr Pellegrini's guest, madam. You'll be on his bill.'

'All the same, I'd prefer to pay my own.'

'Perhaps I'd better call Mr Pellegrini.' His hand moved to the phone. 'He was quite definite.'

'I don't wish him to be disturbed!' I was aware that my voice had assumed its astringent, no-nonsense, classroom tone.

'Very well, madam.'

The size of the bill gave me quite a jolt. My financial reserves are becoming very low. But I wasn't really concerned – which is strange as I have always been rather careful about money. Money didn't seem important as I was quite unable to see the future except in terms of nightmare and disaster.

'You wish to leave any message for the Pellegrini family, madam?'

'No. I'll be telephoning them later. Perhaps you could please arrange to have my car brought round?'

I felt extraordinarily brisk and businesslike. Waiting, I looked through several morning papers.

Again nothing!

Perhaps the body has still not been found. In this fine weather, players would be unlikely to use the shelter. Perhaps even the police had not thought of looking there? Or perhaps, simply, the death of Henry wasn't of sufficient interest to report in a national newspaper? Still, it had all the makings of a good story. Just right for summer holiday reading. 'Man Battered to Death on Golf-Course. Police Seek School Teacher and Teenage Girl.'

'Miss Edwardes?' a man's voice behind me said. My heart nearly stopped.

But it was only a porter to tell me my car was waiting.

It was going to be another scorcher, and hot weather has always produced in me excitement, tension. Today something was going to happen. If necessary, I must *make* it happen.

The feeling was oddly familiar, and suddenly, as I drove down Park Lane, quite fearless in the heavy traffic, I remembered when I had last experienced the identical sensation: when I knew I was about to steal those bits of flimsy underwear in the store.

Carried relentlessly forward by the traffic, I plunged into the whirlpool of Hyde Park Corner, slowed in the bottleneck of Knightsbridge and managed to pull into a backwater just behind Harrods where I found a space at a meter.

Suddenly, I felt hungry. I went into a small cafe, ordered coffee and a croissant. I glanced through more newspapers. Still nothing. The young waiter who served me, kept looking at me, I fancied, in an odd way. There was something strange about my manner, my appearance? Something suspicious? Did my guilt show? . . . To cover my embarrassment, I took out this letter and began writing again . . .

Later at the post office . . .

Marcello, I ordered another cup of coffee and then looked for a cigarette. I hadn't any matches.

I was wearing the same summer suit I had on the day of the killing. I felt in one of the pockets. A moment later I had a blood-stained handkerchief in my hand. The one I

149

had used to wipe the blood from Dusty's fingers and the club.

The young man, the waiter – I think he was Italian, he called me *signorina* – was standing over me, holding a lighter. He was staring at the handkerchief.

'You have been to the dentist, *signorina*?'

'Dentist?' I stared at him stupidly. 'No, of course not!'

I threw the unlit cigarette into my untouched second cup, put a whole pound on the table and fled . . .

Marcello, from this same post office in Knightsbridge, a few moments ago I called our little one.

Her voice was still heavy with sleep. I must have woken her up and she no doubt thought I was speaking from the adjoining room. 'Hi,' she said. 'Let's have breakfast just the two of us together. I guess Dad won't want to be disturbed for a bit. We won't be the only ones who had a night of love.' She put the last three words in quotes.

'I'm not speaking from the hotel.'

'Then where are you, for goodness sakes?'

'I left, checked out.'

'Checked out!' Suddenly she was wide awake. 'But . . .'

'Listen, darling. I'm not going on the trip around Europe with you. I'm not going to America, either. Don't ask why. I just can't. But I'm very grateful I was asked. Please thank your father for me.'

'You're telling me this is good-bye?'

'Yes, that's it. Darling . . .' I was choking back the tears. 'And Dusty . . .'

'Hey!' she said. 'You can't leave me now. You can't. I need you.'

'No, you don't. You'll see. And listen. Darling, don't worry about anything. Don't worry!' I was afraid someone might be listening in. 'You understand? Good-bye, darling . . .'

'Hey!' she cried, excited. 'Don't hang up. There's something . . .'

150

But I did hang up.

Marcello, I am very frightened. Please don't be anxious if you don't hear from me for a few days, or even at all ... I hope your daughter enjoyed her holiday in the Dolomites. I have never been there. They must be very beautiful. And if you can give my good wishes to your wife, in a way that wouldn't offend her ... she is a very sweet, understanding person. I am sending this express. I see another postal strike is threatened in Italy. I hope it reaches you safely.

Eighteen

'You are feeling well?'

'Thank you, I feel fine.'

'But tired?'

'No, no.'

'Last night you were very restless. You have been working too hard.'

Clara places her cool, slightly antiseptic hand on my forehead. 'Perhaps you have a small temperature. These summer colds! You were sneezing quite a lot yesterday.'

Clara has become wonderfully solicitous. Our mutual interest in the work in progress has brought us closer than for years, and I am having an affair with – of all people – my wife. A possible subject for my next novel? Our new-found harmony is oddly attractive.

Why, then, am I so restless? Because the post is irregular? For the past three days, there has been nothing from England. Why are my collaborators so strangely silent?

I have taken to going to the corner kiosk every afternoon, to buy the English newspapers – at ridiculous prices – as soon as they arrive. But they contain nothing about 'our' crime. I am in a most difficult situation.

Only yesterday, Caesare rang me up – from here in Rome, staying at the Excelsior, naturally! on a quick business trip – to ask how the book is progressing. Rashly, perhaps, I promised a script would be on his desk in three or four weeks.

Perhaps I have been too passive. Perhaps I should have taken some positive steps, made concrete suggestions, to stir things up. For a moment this morning, I even thought of sending an anonymous letter to the British police, or even making an equally anonymous phone call, telling them where to look for the body. But that would possibly lead to inquiries (via Interpol?) in my direction, which could be inconvenient. And I feel Dusty, if possible, must be protected. No, all my instincts, literary and otherwise, suggest to me irresistibly that Miss E is the born victim. So I decided to let things take their course, without any interference from me.

A little while ago, the tapes arrived, Henry's tapes – much delayed by the recent strike. So I at least have something to occupy me, editing, and putting the material into what I consider the appropriate place in the script.

But what will the final chapters be? And Clara puts down my feverish excitement to a common cold!

Days passed, still without any mail. Then, early this morning, the phone rang. Dusty.

'Where are you?' I demanded. 'And where the hell have you been?'

'I've been in Paris, Athens and Istanbul,' she said coolly. 'Now I'm here in Rome. *Ciao!*' Somehow, her tone was subtly different.

'Well, you'd better come over here,' I said. 'Clara's at the clinic.'

'No,' she said. 'It's much too hot. Come where it's air-conditioned. I'm at the Cavalieri.'

'But what's been happening? What about Miss E?'

'We'll talk later,' she said. 'We'll be in the Coffee Shop if you arrive within an hour.'

She hung up.

I showered, dressed and drove out to the Hilton. Why on earth did they build the place, if there had to be another, so far out of town!

Pellegrini and his new wife, Beryl, were exactly as Miss E had described. They were both very polite to me, but, I

153

thought, sizing me up. Dusty, now looking and behaving about five years older, was adopting towards me a sort of proprietorial manner which I found both flattering and provoking.

Beryl has never been to Italy before and of course I tried to live up to my countryman's reputation by paying her compliments and shooting burning glances (returned) in her direction when Pellegrini wasn't looking. The two women are already jealous of each other. With some reason on Beryl's part, I think. Dusty treats her father more like a suitor than a parent. There is one thing, however, distinctly in my favour, as far as he is concerned. I am Italian!

There is chit-chat. Beryl will be spending her afternoon in the hotel's beauty salon. Pellegrini has 'meetings'. (It is a business trip as well as a honeymoon.)

It is decided that we will take cocktails in the bar of the Excelsior (where else?) and dinner in Trastevere. At least I won't have far to get home.

I impatiently await the hamburgers to be consumed, but at last they go their separate ways.

'Okay,' Dusty says. 'Let's go up to my room.'

I follow obediently, as if she had seized my sexual organ.

As soon as the door is closed, she drapes her arms around my neck, presses her body to mine. 'Hullo,' she says, 'I'm very hungry for you.'

Once, long ago when I was very young, in another Roman hotel, an American woman, my very *first* American woman, had said exactly those words in exactly the same tone. She was, I suppose, about forty. I about nineteen. Sexually starved, I had performed gratefully for my supper. I look at Dusty now and wonder what she will be like at forty; about all the weird and unwholesome transformations that can take place in women. About how the sloe-eyed Italian beauty of eighteen can become the 150-

154

pound pasta-eating mama. And the delicious fraulein, *Jasmin*-reading and slim, become a devotee of *schlag-sahne* and formidable felt hats. And how the Quant-dressed, sex-for-the-asking girl from London's King's Road becomes yet another knitting and nappy-obsessed suburban housewife. Still looking at Dusty, I also think about the elaborately coiffeured Miami-based widows I see doing Rome in Amexco coaches.

'What are you thinking about?' she says.

'About why you didn't write earlier. About what happened to Miss E.' The lies one nonchalantly utters!

'I was travelling. I knew I'd be here in a few days. There was no need to write. I don't know what happened to Miss E. She simply walked out on us.'

'But I've got to know more. For the book! I've got to have an end.'

'*Amore.* I've written chapters for you. So has Miss E. So even has Henry. You *did* get the tapes?'

'Yes, yes!'

'So! You're the writer. Concoct a nice juicy end. Look, I even killed Henry for you. What more do you want? It happened just the way Miss E no doubt said.'

'But don't you see, if I wrote it that way, you'd be implicated.'

'I would? If Miss E takes the blame, as she undoubtedly and masochistically wishes?'

She began to take off her dress. In spite of the air-conditioning, I was sweating which for me is very unusual, even during a Roman summer.

She slipped out of the rest of her clothes.

'I'll take a shower if you like,' she said, 'and be very all-over clean and American, but I seem to remember you like a woman's natural scents.'

Scarcely listening, I said, 'But what happens to Miss E?'

'What happens? How should I know? You should have

thought about that before you started cooking your faction, that is if you really *do* care what happens to her at all. *Do you?*'

'No.'

'Okay.' She unbuttoned my shirt, loosened the belt of my trousers which descended to my ankles. I could see my reflection in the full-length mirror. Ridiculous.

I stepped, I hoped adroitly, out of them and moved to the bed. I was anxious to get it over with.

Anxious? No, resolved!

But moments later the comic had become farce. For the first time in my life, on a bed with any woman other than my wife, I was utterly unable to perform.

At first, I thought it must be because Clara had been exceptionally passionate. But there have been times, quite recently, when I have been able to make love with two, and on one memorable occasion, even three different women within twenty-four hours; perfectly satisfactorily, indeed, with increasing pleasure.

At first the little one was amused.

'You're tired? You've been working too hard?'

'Perhaps. When I'm busy with a book, I sometimes find it goes better if I don't have sex.'

This isn't true. But it was the kind of explanation I hoped she'd find convincing.

I caressed her, kissed every part of her body. She moaned with pleasure and anticipation.

Nothing!

At last she pushed me away from her and stared at me like a highly unorthodox and appealing inquisitor.

'You have another girl? That's why?'

'No, no.'

I was able to say this with conviction because Clara, a wife, didn't count, and the little one, anyway, had been firmly convinced on her last visit to Rome that Clara and I

156

were simply good friends who happened to eat together and share a very large and chaste bed.

Frankly, I could not think of any plausible explanation – except that, as she straddled my legs and gazed down at me, I saw her hitting that unknown Englishman, our victim, again and again with a blood-stained golf club.

Suddenly, she said, 'You like Beryl? You think she's sexy?'

'I don't know. I haven't thought about her.'

'Liar! You've thought about every woman you've ever met.'

This was a self-evident accusation I could not deny.

'If you want her, all you have to do is put your lips together and blow.'

'That's a good line.'

'Not original. I heard it in an old Bogart movie I saw on TV.'

'I always liked Bogart movies,' I said. 'They don't make them that way any more.'

She said, 'All you have to do is open that door. She'll be back from the beauty parlour any minute.'

'You mean you sleep in connecting rooms?'

'It's a family get-together,' she said. 'Come to think of it, you and Daddy must be around the same age.'

'And both Italian!'

'With rather similar physical characteristics.'

'And may the best man win!' I laughed, but not with amusement. 'You're very mature for your age,' I said.

'Of course. I like playing adult games. I suppose I shouldn't be angry with you. Just patient.'

'Patient?'

'Like Beryl.'

'You listen?'

'I overhear. It's impossible not to. Poor Daddy!'

'But he looks so virile.'

157

'All those pills and potions. He's even cut down on the Scotch. Liquor's supposed to be bad for the sex-drive, isn't it?'

'I'm a moderate wine-drinker myself.'

'Beryl seems to be taking on plenty, though. Did you notice at lunch?'

'Three large whiskies, wasn't it?'

'And it's already showing on her face. She can be puffy around the eyes. Not that you'd notice unless you'd seen her without make-up.'

During this conversation, Dusty had been performing certain intimate manipulations on my person, but entirely without success.

'Okay,' she said at last. 'Let's call it an afternoon. I've read the books. I know it's important for older men to have sex regularly, then they can go on for ages. Which is certainly what I'd want from a husband.'

She said these last words from under the shower, and I wasn't quite sure I had heard her correctly. I went to the bathroom and watched her shivering with pleasure under the assault of the icy water.

'Husband?' I said.

'I thought we'd be married in New York.'

'Married?'

'I can just see the headline. *Italian Author, 50, Weds Girl 18.*'

'But you're seventeen!' The only remark I could think of, under the circumstances.

'I'll be eighteen by the time your book appears. Perhaps we could marry on the actual day of publication. Daddy has lots of friends on Madison Avenue. He could jet-propel the publicity. Would you hand me a towel?'

'Dusty,' I said, 'even under the present state of Italian law, Clara would never agree to a divorce. She's Catholic.'

'Everything can be fixed,' she said. 'And everyone. Daddy's a lawyer, remember. The best.'

158

'Perhaps Daddy wouldn't exactly approve of me as a son-in-law.'

'Oh, he's already agreed. After all, I've been very understanding about Beryl. He thinks I need a sort of father-figure. And I agree. Young men bore me. He's very anxious to read your book.'

'You've told him about the book?' I was astonished.

'Well, naturally. He thinks it's a pity you haven't made it yet internationally, or at least in the States. But, not to worry, he has friends in publishing, too.'

'He knows *your* party in the story? That it's fact?'

Dusty, naked, walked back into the bedroom, poured herself a whisky from a bottle taken from her suitcase ('Daddy disapproves!'), lit a cigarette, began brushing her hair and watched me through the mirror as I began getting into my clothes.

'*Fiction!*' she said. '*Amore*, you're developing the least bit of a paunch. It will vanish when you stop eating so much pasta.'

'But I like pasta!' I almost shouted at her. 'What d'you mean, fiction? Did you murder that Englishman, or didn't you?'

'Let's not be bitchy about the unfortunates,' she said. 'There, but for the grace of God, and so on...'

I watched her brushing her hair with slow, rhythmical, determined strokes.

Suddenly I was bored. With Rome, life in Trastevere, bored even with the 'new' Clara. I was even bored with the idea of writing a book that would appeal to Caesare.

But if I were to return to New York, my favourite hell? A whole new vista of experience, beside a teenage bride, opened before me.

'Of course,' Dusty was saying, 'if the book shouldn't be a success, Daddy could help in other directions. And there's always Beryl.'

Plots for future novels, like rats chasing their own tails in the cages of vivisectionists, were already whirling in my brain.

Dusty put aside the hair-brush and stood up. Again she pressed her body against mine. 'So you see, we could have a very successful marriage. Even if, in time, it turns out to be only a family/business relationship.'

'Which includes Beryl?'

'Beryl and I,' she said, 'have an understanding.'

I wondered just what had happened between London, Paris, Athens, Istanbul and Rome.

'Just what happened between you and Miss E in England?' I said. 'I mean sexually?'

'Apart from the fact that she was crazy about me, nothing. Nothing at all.'

I let the lie pass. I had Miss E's letter, and preferred her as a witness. No, not a witness. An involved party.

Dusty suddenly untwined her arms from my neck and disappeared for a moment into the adjoining bedroom.

Standing again before me, she held out both arms, fists clenched, like a child playing a guessing-game.

'Which?'

I tapped the left one.

On her palm glowed about twenty bright orange capsules.

'The very latest thing,' she said. 'From the most expensive doctor in New York.'

'Some miracle drug?'

'I overheard Daddy and Beryl discussing them, hopefully, last night.'

'He won't miss them?'

'Oh, he's got heaps. For himself *and* his friend. I just did a little juggling with the contents of the two bottles – no one will miss twenty or so. I'll wrap them in a tissue for you. One a day. It takes a little time.'

'Beryl must be getting very excited,' I said. 'Who's this friend?'

160

'Oh, just some sort of business contact. In Palermo. Sicily. Daddy's flying there and back tomorrow.'

I was about to ask Dusty more about this Sicilian friend when Beryl, magnificently coiffured, fingers flashing diamonds, appeared at the connecting door.

'You look beautiful,' I said, dutifully.

'And so do you, sir!' she said, taking in my somewhat dishevelled appearance. 'Dusty's been keeping you entertained?'

Did I only imagine there was a conspiratorial glance between them?

Nineteen

Marcello,

Everyone is very kind here, but I think the woman in the next bed has been warned not to be too talkative. She keeps trying to start a conversation, but stops guiltily when a nurse approaches. I have a strange sense of floating. I suppose I have been under sedation, perhaps still am. When I awoke I seemed to be somewhere between the bed and the ceiling, looking down at myself. There was a fat Chinaman sitting at the foot of the bed, chuckling silently, nodding and smiling benignly, as if he understood everything. But as I slowly descended into my body, he disappeared. But the smile remained, rather like the smile of the cat in *Alice*. But I don't suppose you've read *Alice in Wonderland*, have you, Marcello?

When a young Pakistani nurse brought me tea a little time ago, I said, 'Where's Halfi?'

'Halfi?' She smiled her incomprehension. 'Now who would Halfi be? How are you feeling now? The leg's comfortable?'

'Leg?' I said.

'You're lucky,' she said. 'No broken bones. You'll be right as rain in a few days.'

For the first time since coming round, I became aware of my leg, that I had difficulty in moving it.

'I was in some kind of accident?'

'Nothing to worry about. Now drink your tea.'

She smoothed my pillow.

'But how long have I been here?'

'Just a few days.'

Memories came flooding back. Had I been talking under

anaesthetic or under drugs? Suddenly, I was in a panic. What kind of a hospital was I in? A *prison* hospital? The word was on my lips, but I could not say it. I tried indirect tactics.

'Could I see a newspaper?'

'Now what would you be wanting to see a newspaper for?' the little nurse said in her Pakistani–Irish accent. 'Just relax. Take things easy.'

'What day of the week is it?'

'Now what does that matter? Just drink your tea.'

'But my friends – they'll be worried if they don't know where I am.'

'You don't be upsetting yourself. There'll be plenty of time for letters. Try and sleep.'

She smoothed my pillow again and was gone.

'*Psst!*'

It was the woman in the next bed, alert, conspiratorial, watchful.

'What is it?'

'I've got plenty of paper and envelopes. Don't you worry about *them*. Here!'

She passed a writing-pad over to me as if she were performing some kind of conjuring trick.

'Thanks.'

'Any time.'

'What hospital am I in?'

'St Catherine's! Kensington. The batty wing.'

'The what?'

'They think we're crazy. But of course we know better, don't we! It's they who should be lying here!'

So I wasn't in prison. Just a mental ward!

Apart from the leg injury, just what was I suffering from? Loss of memory?

Actually, Marcello, everything now is very clear. I remember rushing out of that cafe in Knightsbridge, going to the Post Office, talking to Dusty, writing to you. And then

163

I remember walking along Brompton Road, looking in the shop windows.

There was a boutique displaying Italian silk dresses in 'dazzling colours designed to glow just for you alone under a Mediterranean sun'. And of course I was thinking of you. But I saw *his* reflection in the window. *Click!* It was as if he had taken my photograph, and he smiled, his teeth very white against his dark skin. He wore a beautifully tailored mohair suit; there were rings on his fingers. Some Middle Eastern pasha?

I went into the boutique, tried on one of the dresses, which suited and fitted me perfectly, I thought. I paid by cheque, hoping it wouldn't bounce. (Is Mr Askey *still* my friend?)

'I'll wear it,' I said.

The *vendeuse* carefully folded my old suit with the blood-stained pocket-lining into one of the boutique's psychedelic carrier-bags.

He was still there when I emerged, still smiling.

'Very, very nice!' he said, like Peter Sellars doing his oriental thing.

And he fell into step beside me as if he had been my companion for days, like a friendly dog that had attached himself to me.

Marcello, I have no clear recollection of how we spent the rest of the morning, or the afternoon. But around six o'clock, we were in the bar of some West End hotel, drinking whisky and eating salted nuts.

It was only then that he said his name was Halfi.

'And may I have the honour to know yours?' he asked, offering a cigarette of strange fragrance from a gold case, lit by a gold lighter.

'Dusty!' I said. 'Dusty Pellegrini.'

'You are Italian?'

'American of Italian origin,' I said, using the American accent I had acquired during my 'Middle West' period, and

164

automatically adopted during my association with the real Dusty.

'You are a tourist?' he inquired politely.

'A "Visitor to Britain",' I said. 'Last month I was in Rome.'

'Last month I also was in Rome. It was very hot.'

'Yes, very!'

'Which is why I came to London. But here it is also very hot.'

'One cannot escape,' I said.

'It is my ambition to spend a winter in a very cold, very damp climate. Hamburg has been recommended.'

'Hamburg, I would think, would be very cold and very wet. Especially in January.'

'A friend of mine was in Hamburg last winter. He described to me how he sat in the restaurant of a ship moored for the winter at the St Pauli landing-stage, and watched the river Elbe flow past, very thick with ice and very poetic. He was eating leg of goose with red cabbage, a local speciality.'

'It must have been quite an experience.'

'Hamburg is said to be a very naughty city,' he said. 'But I do not think it can be more naughty than London.'

'Naughtier!' I said, always the schoolmarm.

'Thank you. I am anxious to improve my English.'

He ordered another round.

'You are perhaps engaged this evening?'

'I was thinking of going to the theatre, or perhaps the cinema.'

'Alone?'

'Why not?'

'You American ladies! So independent! Perhaps you will do me the honour of spending the evening with me?'

'All right,' I said, 'thank you,' and added, for no apparent reason, 'my father is a lawyer.'

'And I am a gentleman,' he said, bowing slightly, with

deference.

We did not go to the theatre or the cinema, Marcello. We went, obviously, to an Italian restaurant, specialising in *frutta di mare* which we ate, you remember, so often in Rome? We drank Frascati. Too much Frascati! The food was served by young men in white jeans and blue-and-white jerseys who burst into Neapolitan songs at the pop of a cork.

The food was prepared at the table, which I know is gastronomically unsound. Cooking is best done in the kitchen. Yes, I know. But still I said, encouragingly, 'I love it when food is served as a sort of rite.'

'In the Middle East that is the custom. I think, perhaps, that you are not a typical American?'

'Second generation,' I said. 'I came over on an Italian boat, New York to Naples, eating Italian all the way, and loving it.'

He looked puzzled. 'You don't look Italian.'

'Well, America's a melting pot. Mother was Brooklyn Irish, but Dad's the predominant influence.'

By the time we left the restaurant, I was more than a little tight. In the taxi, I discovered I had lost my purse. In the hotel bar? In some taxi? We went back to the restaurant. No purse. It didn't matter. Finally, we arrived at a night-club in some cellar. Still nothing mattered, even what had, or had not, happened to Henry.

Halfi ordered something that was supposed to be champagne. It was alcoholic, anyway. Hand in hand, we watched the nudes. There was one act especially: two women. Watching it, I could scarcely breathe. Two bodies flowing over and around one another, entwining, serpentine, finally fused in imitation (could it possibly have been genuine?) ecstasy. The sight of it tormented me unbearably. I needed somebody. Now. Anybody.

I was aware that Halfi was watching *me*, not the activities on the tiny stage.

166

I said, 'You want to take me home?'

He smiled as politely as at our first encounter, outside the boutique.

'You are staying at which hotel?'

'Your home,' I said.

'But where are you staying?'

'Last night I was at the Hilton. But I checked out.'

'So you have nowhere to go?'

'Why are you so obtuse?' I said.

He signalled the waiter and asked for the bill.

There was no taxi, so we walked a little. On to Charing Cross Road, with its shops, literary and medical, catering for the more unorthodox sexual needs. Halfi was interested.

I said, 'Why does sex, any kind of sex, have to be sordid? Why does it have to do with lonely men emerging from hotel rooms and picking up a tart? Why does it have to be *dirty*?'

My voice must have risen. He didn't want to know me.

'You think I'm a tramp, I just want your money?'

Two men, one a Negro, stopped to stare and grin. The Negro said, 'Oh, baby, baby, baby, come tramp with me!'

Halfi looked as if he wanted to disappear on his oriental magic carpet into the thin air of the Soho night. But somehow he still managed to smile, waving to every passing taxi. They all had their flags down.

I grabbed his arm. 'You do, don't you? You think I'm a whore?'

'I think you are a very nice lady,' he said politely.

'Of course I'm nice! But I still want you to take me home!'

'Oh, baby, baby!' the Negro said. 'Come home with me!'

At last a taxi glided to the kerb. Halfi opened the door.

'You first,' I said. 'You don't get rid of me so easily.'

'I'm going to find you a hotel.'

'You first!'

167

Two police women came up then, both young, freshly scrubbed, solemn, official. A blonde and a brunette, one fat, one thin. A sort of Scotland Yard comedy-duo.

They looked me over, disapprovingly.

'Is this woman annoying you?' the fat blonde said to Halfi.

'Am I annoying you, Halfi?' I said.

Halfi was speechless.

'If she is annoying you, sir, please say so,' the thin brunette said.

I liked the 'sir' bit. Proper respect for an obvious, well-heeled, mohair-suited visitor to Britain!

Halfi's smile became increasingly enigmatic.

'You do *speak* and *understand* English, sir?'

Slightly condescending. That did it.

'Oh yes. Of course I speak English. Naturally!'

'Well, then, sir? About this woman...'

'I don't want any trouble. No trouble at all.'

'But she was annoying you?' The thin brunette put her hand on my arm.

'You're going to let them arrest me, Halfi?' I said. He appeared baffled. 'Under the Street Offences Act,' I said. 'For soliciting. Prostitution.'

'But the lady's American,' Halfi said, mystified.

The two ladies of the law exchanged somewhat non-plussed glances.

'You *are* American, madam?' the fat blonde said. 'A visitor to this country?'

'Yes, I am indeed!' I said in my best 'Dusty' accent, 'and my father is a very famous, very efficient and very expensive criminal lawyer.'

'Where are you staying, madam?' the thin brunette said.

'The Hilton.'

'Could we see your passport, please?'

'No, you couldn't. It's at the hotel.'

168

The fat blonde said to Halfi, 'You do wish to make a complaint, sir?'

The taxi-driver who had been listening to the whole exchange with a sort of bored tolerance, said, 'Sir, this delay is costing you money.'

'Oh, baby, baby, baby!' the black man said, and began to dance.

Two or three other interested spectators joined the group.

'A nice thing,' I said, 'if a gal spending good U.S. dollars here gets picked on by two female cops, just because she's having a friendly argument with her boy-friend! The Ambassador happens to be a friend of mine!'

The blonde and the brunette were beginning to look really worried.

I looked at Halfi. 'Well,' I said, 'you want me arrested or not? After what I thought was a pleasant evening? Yes or no?' I was astonished by my glibness.

'The lady,' Halfi said, 'is my friend. I am taking her home.'

'Hooray!' the black man said.

'And where,' the taxi-driver wanted to know, 'is home?'

'Kensington,' Halfi said.

Suspicious, the blonde and brunette watched us drive off in the taxi...

Looking back, I saw the Negro trying, unsuccessfully, to dance with the fat blonde.

Marcello, I had to break off. After lunch of soup, fish and mashed potatoes, tinned fruit and custard, I had a visitor. A man in a raincoat, though the sun streams into the ward. He is, I suppose, about fifty, and fatherly. Not at all intimidating, for a police officer.

'Well, now, how are you feeling?'

'Better, thank you.'

'The leg's quite comfortable?'

'Oh yes, quite!'

'Oh, good! Well, there are just a few questions, that is, if you feel ... ?'

So this was it!

'Questions?'

He was looking at my left hand and its lack of wedding ring. 'It's "Miss", isn't it?'

'Edwardes,' I said. 'Elizabeth.'

'And your address?'

I gave him the address of my cottage near Brighton.

'Brighton, eh? Very nice! I had a day by the sea there, just a few weeks ago. With the wife and kids, of course.'

'Of course!' I echoed, aware, even in this day and age, of the Prince Regent, sexy week-end, implications.

'You know, you're quite the mystery woman.'

'Mystery woman?'

'Well, you were talking with an American accent when they brought you in.'

This, no doubt, was the softening up process.

'How long have I been here?'

'Four days.'

So Dusty would be goodness-knows-where in Europe! Away, out of it!

'So he's been found!' I said.

'Found?' He looked puzzled, 'Now who would that be? A man you were running away from?'

'Well, Henry Walton, of course!'

'And you were running away from this gentleman just before it happened?'

'I suppose you could say that, yes.'

'And you can give me the address of this Mr Walton?'

'Of course.' I watched his pencil moving.

'But that's in the north of England!'

'Obviously.'

'And he was here, with you? In London?'

The man in the mac was trying to trap me into a confession. Why bother?

170

I said, 'North or south, Henry Walton's dead, and I killed him.'

For a long time the man in the mac just looked at me. Then he said, 'I see! So that's why you tried to kill yourself?'

'*I* tried to kill myself?' I was astonished.

'That was the way it looked to the witnesses.'

'Witnesses? I don't remember any witnesses.'

'So you don't remember the accident?'

'No. But I suppose that's how my leg got hurt ... I remember...'

'Yes?'

'Well, I remember shouting something at Halfi and then running out ...'

'Halfi?' the man in the mac said patiently. 'Who's Halfi?'

'I don't know his other name. I didn't ask. He came from the Lebanon or Egypt or Saudi Arabia, somewhere like that ... I'm terribly tied. I'd like to rest now, if you don't mind.'

'Good idea!' he said, and stood up. 'Try not to worry. About anything.'

The nurse came and gave me another pill and made sure I swallowed it.

I pretended to sleep. But when I was sure no one was watching, I started to finish this letter to you, Marcello. It seems terribly important to do so.

The woman in the next bed says she's leaving tomorrow. She's not going to stay in a place where everyone hates her. She says she'll post the letter as soon as she gets out. Isn't that kind, Marcello? I do appreciate kindness in people...

I can't write any more now. I really am feeling most awfully sleepy...

Twenty

I have just typed out Miss E's last letter which, needless to say, delighted me. Very little editing was necessary – I left her dialogue practically untouched. Her ear for English conversation is, no doubt, more reliable than mine. With American dialogue I am more at home of course; but I have never been to England which is one of those countries which remains the more fascinating to me simply because it exists entirely in my imagination.

Our self-created plot is proceeding to its inevitable, but as yet unforeseeable end. My biggest worry now is that I shall not hear from Miss E again, as may well happen if she pleads guilty to murder. But then, presumably, the case will be fully reported in the English press.

Of course I am sorry for her. But after all she will have got what she always wanted: punishment. She will be the victim of her own sense of sin. An innocent criminal, a criminal innocent – kind, gentle, well-meaning – but condemned. A Kafka-like creature from life whom I groomed to act out a destiny to which, until I entered her life, she was aspiring but which, without my encouragement, she would never have achieved.

She will, I hope and believe, be fulfilled, even in a way happy, in the mad-house in which she will no doubt be confined.

Clara, from her professional standpoint, agrees that as a frustrated lesbian she would never be able to come to terms with herself, except possibly after long treatment. She also agrees that the book is almost finished. I have not of course shown Clara all the script – particularly those parts which contain references to her; and she is not aware of Dusty's true role. I am experiencing slight but insistent feelings of regret that soon I shall be parting from her, and plunging, permanently this time, into my New York hell. I shall miss her cool intellect and – words it would have been impossible for me to write only a few short months ago – I shall also miss her physical presence, her body.

The truth, incredibly, is that at the moment I can only make love with her. Almost every night she displays a passion and ingenuity which seem limitless. I am still asleep at ten, even eleven, exhausted by the activities of the night; but when I finally arise from our bed of love, it is to find her, serene and smiling, cooking me a nourishing breakfast – for of course she has heard me getting up and stumbling about the bedroom.

The little American is patient and I try to 'satisfy' her in other ways, but unless I am able to perform properly soon, my future life with her will be something of a problem. I have tried everything. I took her to a cheap hotel; the house of a friend; even to a bordello whose madame is an acquaintance of mine. All in the hope that novel surroundings would stimulate me. To no avail. But plainly she is now beginning to regard me as a business and social as much as a sleeping partner. What an odd twist of fate! Would the orange capsules help?

We met this afternoon, lying in bed but without even attempting sex, and planned our departure. And future. We agreed to book an Alitalia flight to New York in just two weeks. I am to take over to the Hilton only a few essential clothes and papers, a little at a time, so as not to arouse Clara's suspicions.

Our arrival will be marked by a party thrown by her father at the Plaza to which gossip columnists and publishing and film personalities will of course be invited.

Daddy has already secured a promise from a New York publisher that he will bring out the book, but there is a proviso in the agreement that causes me misgivings: that

173

he, the publisher, at his discretion, may arrange for any re-writing he may deem necessary to improve the work's commercial possibilities. I am to complete my draft in New York – Daddy has already leased for us a Central Park West apartment, as a wedding present – in consultation with the publisher's editorial staff. Ominous! But that's the trouble with faction. Any industrial product tends to become the creation of a team. I am already beginning to feel a loss of identity. Do I really want to be married to this teenage monster whom, at least in part, I have created? But can I afford to reject the opportunities she offers? Would it be more cowardly to go with her? Or to remain?

I am as worried about my future as a writer as I am about my capacity to attract women which, I confess, was largely due to my sexual prowess. Women have always been both my raw material as a writer and an endless source of amusement to me as a man.

I must try to repel Clara's nightly assaults. She is draining too much of my energy... All my life I have had a horror of drugs. But the orange capsules glow temptingly, like forbidden gems. To take or not to take – that is the question.

Twenty-one

Marcello,

The woman in the next bed, Mrs Davies, was not allowed to leave today, but her husband came to visit her, a small man with a hunted look, who promised to post my last letter.

I do hope you received it. Mrs Davies will give him this one to post on his next visit, the day after tomorrow.

Marcello, writing is very difficult. I feel I am always under observation. I have been questioned at length by a woman I think must be a psychiatrist. Of course I was as evasive as possible, saying nothing at all about you or our little American.

Found 'fit', I suppose I'll be formally charged, as a result of my confession, and taken to prison. The prospect frightens me. But at least there will be no more uncertainty. My chief worry is not being able to communicate, with you. I hope my letters *are* posted. I haven't a bean, even for stamps. But Mrs Davies says not to worry.

I said I was frightened, but that isn't strictly true – though I ought to be, I suppose. Actually, I'm quite relaxed. No doubt because of the drugs they're giving me. My memory is coming back. At first I couldn't remember exactly what happened before I was brought here. But now I do remember. I should feel shame? But I don't. The drugs, no doubt.

Where was I? I told you about my encounter with the police women? And going off with Halfi? In the taxi?

We drove to his flat, just off Kensington High Street. (He wanted to put me down at a hotel, but I refused to get out of the cab.) It was a small, one-room 'bachelor' place, on the ground floor of what had once been a Victorian family house. There was an Indian restaurant, aromatic with curry, almost next door, which Halfi said he frequently patronised, which I can well believe. His breath was piquant with betel-nut and exotic spices.

Ah, I was about to enter a new world, strange and oriental, in which all my hang-ups would disappear! The sultan's palace of W. 8!

There was a divan with crumpled sheets in one corner, threadbare chairs, piles of back numbers of *The Economist* and *The Statesman and Nation*. A TV and a number of empty bottles. And a record-player.

Halfi said the place actually belonged to a Syrian friend who was studying, on a government grant, at the London School of Economics, and writing a thesis on the Social and Political History of Oil in the Middle East. The friend, apparently, was on holiday somewhere in Spain.

'And what are you studying?' I asked.

He handed me a glass of Algerian. I was already, as you will have gathered, quite tight. He probably thought a little more would make me easier to handle.

'Sociology,' he said.

'And what's your thesis?'

'Sex and Colour in Britain.'

'You've had a coloured girl here in Britain? I mean, you've done field research?'

He looked uncomfortable, non-committed.

'I'm not coloured, unless white's a colour. But I'm a girl.'

He said, 'It is very late. Thank you for a very pleasant time. Please will you not let me phone an hotel?'

'I haven't any luggage,' I said. 'Hotels don't like people without luggage. What's wrong with the divan?'

I put on a record. Greek bouzouki, I think it was. I turned the volume up and began to make the steps – memories of a package holiday at Sounion!

'Not so loud, please. Or I will have unpleasantnesses with

176

the landlady!'

'You don't like trouble? You don't like to be in a spot, Halfi? With a coloured girl? An English girl, an American girl, or any kind of girl?'

I didn't want him. I didn't really want any man. But I had to know if a man, even Halfi, could want *me*. Whether I was capable of arousing desire. It was my last chance.

I began to unzip the Italian silk dress. Sitting on the divan, he stared at me, fascinated. But terrified. I went close to him. I took his hands and placed the palms upon my body. I whispered, cried to him for love. I guided his fingers to free me from what remained of my clothing.

I stood before him naked. Nothing . . . nothing. I was an idolatress trying vainly to bring a stone image to life.

At last, desperate, humiliated, I backed away from him to the fireplace. There was a large mirror over it, Marcello, and in the dim light I stared at myself, saw my face bathed in sweat, hair dishevelled, in my eyes nightmare, and beyond, Halfi, still sitting there on the divan, still watching me. Desperately I wanted not him, I wanted Dusty. My fingers sought my own sex and he watched, his eyes hard and clinical now, as if I were a specimen of a rare, unnatural kind. And as the forbidden pleasure grew his eyes also grew as they held mine in the mirror. His lips seemed to form words, the corners of his mouth twitched. Then, before I reached a climax, he began to laugh, at first silently, then out loud. I tore my eyes from his and then I saw his thesis on the table, next to the typewriter, within arm's reach. A second later, my fingers were touching the paper, pages and pages covered with the workings of a small, meticulous, crabbed, unemotional hand, and suddenly it was I who was laughing, wildly, hysterically, tossing some of the pages into the air, tearing others with fingers wet with the scent of my own body. Some I threw towards the gas-fire (which he had lighted because the night was cold), and suddenly the room was brighter,

177

raining with glowing scraps of thesis. He was upon me then, with a different kind of passion, shouting incoherently in a language I didn't understand, trying to rescue what was left of his contribution to human knowledge and put out the fire at the same time. I was laughing as we struggled, Marcello, laughing. My fingers found the neck of the bottle of Algerian, still half-full, and I hit him with it, the wine running down my arm and over my body, and then I was making for the door and the last I saw of him as I glanced back, he was on his hands and knees, his face red with the grape, swaying like a drunken crazy man, clawing at the papers burning in the grate. And then the night air, cool on my body, and I was running. I saw the lights of the approaching car and ran towards them, as if for sanctuary, and there was a screaming, tearing sound, and sudden violent pain and then red oblivion, filled with strange shapes and phantoms and Dusty and you, Marcello ... until I came round in this ward for the mad ...

The woman psychiatrist has just come into the ward, Marcello. If I cannot write to you again, good-bye ... good-bye. Do what you like with what I have written. Do *you* think I'm mad? Marcello, I know you're not a Catholic, but will you pray for me? ... Buy the English papers, then perhaps you'll find out what they do to me. Mrs Davies says hurry, so I'm passing this and the envelope to her. I do hope her husband ...

Twenty-two

'Cream and sugar?'

'Thank you.'

'And what about one of those buns? With jam?'

'They do look rather good.'

'I think I'll have one myself. I don't suppose you ate much in there?'

'No, not much. You're very kind. It was good of you to find my car. I'd no idea where I'd left it.'

'Well, it found its way to the police pound, of course. No trouble.'

'So I'll have to pay an enormous fine.'

'Oh, we're forgetting that one, the circumstances being ...'

'A little unusual.'

'Coffee all right?'

'Fine. They always gave me tea in there. Coffee makes a pleasant change.'

'Yes, I expect so.'

'You must be a very busy man. I appreciate your meeting me the way you did. It must be unusual for someone in your position to contact again someone like me who ...'

'Well, perhaps. But I thought you might want to ask me a few questions for a change.'

'Questions?'

'I mean about things that might still be troubling you. And about people.'

'You mean about Henry?'

'He'd be included of course.'

'I still can't understand it. I mean why he isn't dead? You've actually seen him?'

'Not personally. But two officers of the local C.I.D. have.'

'And he's quite all right?'

'Well, his head was bandaged and he appeared to be rather the worse for drink. He was under a strain of course, but that was natural, I suppose.'

'Natural?'

'His mother had just died.'

'Oh? I suppose I should say I'm sorry. She had cancer.'

'Apparently. It would be what they call a happy release. Anyway, it made questioning him a little awkward just then.'

'Yes, I suppose so. But they did ask him about the bandages?'

'He said he fell down the wine-cellar stairs. It's an old house. Spooky.'

'Yes. I wouldn't want to live there. Never!'

'The way you said that, the possibility existed?'

'We're supposed to be engaged, waiting for Mother to die.'

'And now?'

'No. It's off.'

'He knows that?'

'He'll guess.'

'You've known Henry quite some time, I take it.'

'About eight years. I was born up there.'

'The Waltons are a well-known family, it seems.'

'They owned one of the biggest mills, until King Cotton was dethroned.'

'Odd sort of engagement, lasting all that time.'

'Henry's an odd sort of man. But then I'm an odd sort of woman. Could I have another coffee?'

'Of course.'

'You probably know the police have been interested in him before. Something to do with a girl who worked in the mill before it was closed down. She said she'd been . . .'

'Raped? Yes, I heard that. The girl withdrew the charge.'

'You believe him capable of that sort of thing?'

'I don't know anything about anybody any more.'

'You weren't the only house-guest there, I believe.'

'I was there with a friend.'

'A very good-looking young American girl. The house-keeper says Henry and this girl were very friendly.'

'One can't believe everything Hannah says. She's a bit potty and she doesn't like me. All she'll want now that Mrs Walton's gone is to stay on in the house and look after him.'

'I see. You happen to know where your young American friend is now?'

'She's travelling somewhere on the Continent, with her parents. Does it matter?'

'Not really. Seeing Henry insists he fell down the cellar stairs. Anyway, whatever happened, or didn't happen, it seems to have cleared the air ... Ah, here's the coffee. One lump, isn't it?'

'Thank you. Cleared the air? I suppose you mean, ended my engagement?'

'Well, yes, if that's what you wanted. And I suppose it is. After all, murder, even if it's only in the imagination, is pretty definite, a sort of final solution. Well, I'll have to be running along. You have that letter to your local hospital?'

'Yes, yes of course.'

'Don't forget it, will you?'

'I'll try not to.'

'A psychiatrist is no one to be afraid of. I suppose all of us could use one, sometime or another.'

'You know, when I was in the lift on my way out of hospital, I wished it would keep on going down and never stop until it came out in another world.'

'Like Australia, for instance? Have you ever thought of going abroad, making a completely fresh start?'

'Yes, I tried that. In America. And in Italy. Rome.'

'Really? Well, it doesn't always work. Now don't forget

181

that letter, will you?'

'I won't forget.'

'That's a promise?'

'I promise I won't forget about the letter.'

'Good. Just finish your coffee. Take it slowly on the way home.'

'Yes. What I was trying to say is that, if you hadn't been there waiting for me when the lift gates opened, I don't know what I'd have done. You know, ever since I was a child I've been afraid of policemen. Isn't that an odd confession from the carefully-brought-up daughter of a clergyman? And here I am talking to one as if he were an old friend.'

'I'd like you to think of me as a friend, Miss Edwardes. You know, it's funny, some of the people I've arrested talked, I mean really talked, to me for the first time in their lives. A pity, really. A lot of people don't seem to find anyone to talk to.'

'What about Henry?'

'What about him?'

'Well, what's he got to look forward to, in that mausoleum, with his cigarette cards and his gadgets?'

'I'd say he's no longer your concern, Miss Edwardes. You imagined him dead. Let him stay dead, anyway, for you. Try to keep busy, that's the secret. Now, if you'd like to talk to me anytime when you happen to be in London . . . Here's my number.'

'Yes, thank you. I don't know how to thank you, I wouldn't know how to begin.'

'Don't try. A very interesting case really. One for the book!'

'The book?'

'Oh, just a turn of phrase. You're all right now?'

'If it wasn't so hot. I wish it would rain.'

'It will. Nothing lasts for ever.'

The tar on the road oozed like glue, and the tyres made a

sticky, swishing, wet sound. I cried all the way, a damp tissue clutched in my hand.

My little house was very quiet, very still. The first thing I saw in the hall was an Italian silk scarf Dusty had forgotten. I pressed it to my face and it still had traces of her perfume.

My head was splitting. The hospital had given me a few capsules. Sedatives, not more than three a day, and I had already had two. Perhaps a cup of tea would help, if only because to make tea was performing a familiar, reassuring routine.

I went into the kitchen and let the water run before filling the kettle. I held my hands under the water and then wet my face. The wire round my skull seemed to become tighter and tighter. I looked out of the window, at the overgrown garden, the grass thick after weeks of neglect, the molehills rampant, like acts of sabotage. Earlier in the summer, I had thought of calling in a mole-catcher, but the thought of animal-murder on my own land appalled.

I turned on the gas, match-box unused in my hand, looked out over the garden and listened to the hiss of gas, yet did not listen.

There was something strange about the garden. For a few seconds, I could not think what it was. And then I knew. The light was different, the sun had gone. The heat was still there, but clouds were piling up.

Sun or rain. What did it matter? Why not finish the whole miserable business? There would simply be just one less of the diminishing race of unmarried, slightly comic, superfluous, non-pill-taking spinsters, a doomed breed, anyway. And who would shed a single tear? The gas hissed hypnotically.

The sudden jangle of the phone broke the spell. Quickly, guiltily, I lit the gas and put on the kettle as if I had been caught – again! – in a criminal anti-social act.

'Miss Dutton-Smith!'

'Elizabeth? I've been trying to get in touch with you for days. Where *have* you been?'

'Abroad. Rome, actually.'

'In August? Much too hot!'

'Yes, it was rather. But then it's hot here, too.'

There must have been tears in my voice.

'You're all right?'

'Oh yes. Perfectly, thank you. I'm simply . . .'

'Yes?'

'Well, glad that you called. I mean now, at this particular moment.'

'I've been worried about you.'

'Oh, no need to worry, really. You're having a good holiday?'

'No. I hate holidays. You have my letter?'

'Letter?' I had not bothered to look at the pile of paper that had collected behind the front door during my absence. 'No. I only came into the house a few minutes ago. I haven't opened anything yet!'

'Oh well, never mind. The thing is, have you done anything about a job?'

'No. No, I haven't. I don't suppose I could arrange anything to do with teaching anyway.'

'Well, I couldn't do anything for you at my school. But I've just spent an excruciating week with an old friend in the West Country, the head of a so-called "progressive" school. I told her about your little "exploit" – shall we call it? – and she didn't seem to mind a bit. Quite the contrary. I think she may have a place for you. If you're interested . . . Hullo? Are you there?'

'Miss Dutton-Smith,' I managed to say at last, 'I'm extremely grateful. I can't even begin to say how much. In the West Country? May I think about it?'

'Yes. But not for too long. My friend has to make her plans for the winter term. I'll have to let her know. She's an interesting woman. Unmarried, very independent. I think

184

you'd get on well. The school caters especially for the odd children of odd parents. You'd probably find it quite a challenge.'

'But Miss Dutton-Smith, do you really think I'm fit to be a teacher?'

'But of course you are! Teachers don't have to be saints or nuns. Anyway, you're a good one, and good ones are rare. If you didn't teach, it would be a horrible waste. And waste is something I personally abhor. Do you like spaghetti?'

'Spaghetti? Well, yes, I do rather.'

'I thought, having been in Italy, you'd be sick of pasta. But on Sundays I usually indulge. With lots of sauce Bolognaise. And Chianti, of course!'

'I'd love to come.'

'Good. That's settled then.'

Marcello, I drank my tea, I swallowed my aspirin. I sat at the kitchen table and looked over the letters. I read the one from Miss Dutton-Smith which contained the news I had just learned over the phone. There were bills. A bank statement – balance less than £50. Circulars. Postcards from girls I had taught, from Scotland, Brittany, Ireland, Spain. And an envelope in a bold, almost childish hand I recognised at once, the envelope also bearing the rubric Cavalieri Hilton. I held it with fingers suddenly trembling, and tried to decipher the date of posting. Without success.

Sipping my tea, nibbling a biscuit, I looked at the envelope, not opening it, not daring to know what the contents might be. A declaration of love? Or of final dismissal?

The letter lay still unopened on the kitchen table as I washed my cup and saucer and put the biscuit tin back in the cupboard. But it was in my hand as I got again into the little Morris and drove down the lane and on to the main road that led into the town with its familiar shops whose windows contained the promise of happiness if only one wore the right clothes, ate the right foods, swallowed the

185

right patent medicines and washed one's clothes with the right miraculous detergent. I drove past them towards the sea, to the harbour with its twin strong arms which seemed to offer a surer safety.

This Channel town, Marcello, which you have never known, except through my inadequate descriptions, is dead in winter, half dead in spring and autumn, and becomes artificially lively only for a few weeks in summer, with strangers from London, and who-knows-where! A phoney place. But down at the harbour, the reason for the existence of the place, once simply a fishing-village, in the alliance of love and enmity which is land and sea, the honesty remains.

It was the quietest hour, the light going fast. Only a few fishermen, at decent private intervals, stood, almost motionless, at the end of the jetty, self-contained middle-aged or elderly men, watching their lines, waiting for a bite meaning supper, or merely for the moment when it was time to go home.

I parked the car and walked towards them, not as an intruder, but rather as a novitiate, wishing to share their solitude. I have often taken this walk, Marcello, especially in autumn and winter, well-wrapped against the cold. It is so different from your water-fronts and harbours in Italy, with their noise and life and colour. Here, even when there is a good catch, there is no *frutta di mare*, no fish colourful but horrifying (to me) even in death, only squirming flesh whose colour is the colour of the grey, northern sea. In your country, the sun, even at night, is the only reality. Here it is a dream of the day, a promise, seldom a reality. This hot summer has been not a dream but a nightmare. Winter, only weeks away, is the only reality. Or so it seems to be now, as I write this, my last letter.

Great clouds were piling up over the sea and land, and a warm wind rushed in from the west. The long weeks of crazy-making sun were ending. I walked to the very end of the pier. A fishing boat chugged in through the harbour-

186

mouth, the throb of its diesel vanishing almost as soon as it was heard in the rising wind. I looked out across the sea and thought of that day, which I haven't told you about, when Dusty and I drove out of Rome and went to sea at Sperlonga and she appeared to me like a naked goddess, infinitely remote, sailing with me to the ends of the earth.

In that moment, when there was just light enough, I found the courage to read her letter.

'Dearest Liz – so in spite of everything you ran out on me. By now you will have discovered what a little bitch am I, for sure! Don't think too badly of me. Yes, of course, I did it for Marcello. But I did it for you, too. More so! I mean to help you get away from him, in your mind and physically. For good. Finish! So you'd be free to do your own thing. Right? You're with me? Of course a lot of the inspiration came from Marcello, and of course he was using me and, through me, you. But whoever imagined creative people are *moral*? I played my part for kicks. Right! But I guess, deep down, I really thought I was helping you. Is Henry dead? Dead and forgotten? Or at least someone you can't possibly go back to? Liz, it's not for me to tell you what to do with your own life. But do your own thing. Whatever it is. Write, if you want to. Teach, if it would amuse you. And if you want to work up an interest in politics, think about blowing up No 10, Downing Street. And if you want a woman, have her. If you can find the right one. I'm sorry is wasn't me. Apparently, I have to have that particular piece of male flesh inside me. Or it's no go. A rather ridiculous object to base one's life around? I agree. But when it's not limp! Oh, boy! Seriously, Liz, I wanted you to come to the Continent. I wanted you to come to the States. Maybe you'd have found the going smoother there, I don't know. But if you didn't see it that way, well, it's your decision. But one day I hope you'll come

187

over. I guess being up there in Henry's house in the north of England was one of the great experiences of my life. What happened in that spooky building near the ninth tee? Well, I'll tell you! He really did attack me. And I really did attack him, I mean with the putter. I intended murder, or at least a killing in self-defence. Which is the sort of thing Marcello wanted. For his book! Well, I knocked Henry out, but didn't kill him. It's as simple as that.

Liz, I'm writing this just before flying back to the States. Not with Dad or Beryl. Alone! And not with Marcello. You're astonished? I mean that he was supposed to be going back with me anyway? Well, that was the idea. To get married. A big publishing event, to promote his, sorry, your book! So now you see the full extent of my duplicity. And I would have taken him with me, too, if things had worked out differently. But he couldn't make love to me any more. Suddenly! So I said good-bye. No, I didn't say anything, I wrote him a note from Fiumicino, just as I'm writing this one to you. (The plane leaves in ten minutes.) I guess I've had enough of humans for a while. I'll go back to biology, kill a few more rats. But that night in London... Liz, if you ever feel like coming over...'

Marcello, after reading our little one's letter, I felt only pain and humiliation. I was about to tear it up into tiny pieces and throw them into the sea. But then I thought, no. I'll make a copy of the letter and send it to you. Perhaps you'll find it useful? In the script... If it helps you, I'm glad. You have helped me, one way or another, and I'm grateful.

Walking away from the end of the pier, I stopped for a moment to watch a fisherman who had a bite. A very small fish, and I felt sorry for it.

'Not much for supper,' he said, taking it off the hook.

'Throw it back!'

He looked at me quizically, an old man with kindly eyes.

'After standing here waiting for it, for more than three hours?'

'Throw it back,' I said.

He stood looking at me, the fish gasping in his hand. Then he nodded and smiled. Perhaps he was a very wise as well as a very old man.

'Aye!' he said. 'Let it grow!'

And he tossed the little fish back into the sea.

There was rain on my face as I walked away from the end of the pier. Soaking, obliterating, cleansing rain.

Twenty-three

Caesare,

As arranged this morning on the phone, I am sending you the complete file, dossier, manuscript, or whatever you like to call it. I leave it entirely to your discretion to take whatever action (or none) you think best. I am also sending you Miss E's address in case you feel like getting in touch with her, as I hope you will.

The funeral is the day after tomorrow. I will, judging from the number of phone calls I have had from journalists, be a matter of considerable press interest. Marcello was, apparently, a more important literary figure than I had realised; but then, of course, the closer one is to a person the less one appreciates, often, the workings of his inner life. I confess I found many of his books boring – except this last one, which is not really by him at all.

However, you (now that you have the script) and I are the only ones aware of all the facts. Do you think I should go to the police? One has to consider his reputation (one owes him that much!), and obviously his death was not suicide. I feel very confused. If you come to the funeral, I hope you will be able to stay in Rome for a day or so, so that we can discuss the situation in all its implications.

After his death, I took five of the capsules to the laboratory at the hospital. Four of them were completely harmless; a multi-vitamin/hormone pharmaceutical, recently developed in the United States and prescribed to men worried about declining sexual prowess. As a doctor, I believe their possible effect may be more psychological than physical. Be that as it may ...

The fifth capsule contained a cyanide derivative which,

the moment the gelatine dissolved, would be almost instantly lethal.

In view of the circumstances in which Marcello acquired the capsules, as described in the script, it is obvious that, far from wishing to kill himself, he simply wished to satisfy his little American sexually while making a bigger name for himself as a writer in America.

You will of course have seen in the newspapers how a notorious Mafioso, recently exiled from the United States, died in a Palermo villa the other day in circumstances, forensically speaking, exactly similar to those in which Marcello met his end. The possibilities for publicity and scandal (not to mention profit from the book!) are limitless.

Marcello, as you know, had practically come to the end of his financial resources. An ironic situation, is it not? As his widow, I would, presumably, benefit. But, as I am a doctor and I have my daughter to consider, I do not wish to be subjected to a lot of publicity. I leave the handling of the situation to you who are, after all, his literary executor. When we marry, after a decent interval, I wouldn't want the gutter-press to make a meal of me. So be very circumspect, I beg of you. I must stop. The dress-maker has arrived with my weeds.

When you read Marcello's description of my 'passion' for him, please don't be jealous. Most of it is untrue. His was a world of fantasy. An appropriate epitaph? You are my love, my only love ... Clara.